Lords
of the
Archipelago

Blood-Feud

D.B. Motu

LORDS OF THE ARCHIPELAGO: BLOOD-FEUD

First edition. August 2, 2021.

Copyright © 2021 D.B. Motu.

ISBN: 979-8215639320

Written by D.B. Motu.

Table of Contents

Radder scanned the ocean in front of him, following the line of shimmering sun all the way to the blue horizon. Pretty, he thought, like Minecraft snow. The Archipelago stretched as far as the eye could see, a seemingly unending maze of islands, mostly uncharted and uninhabited, surrounded by a million square kilometers of wild blue water. It was absolutely breathtaking, incomparable in scope and raw natural beauty, a wilderness straddling the nautical borders of half a dozen countries—all of whom claimed it and none of whom controlled it.

From what he had heard, the Archipelago was the wild, wild west, complete with legends and monsters, villains and heroes.

Radder could barely take it all in.

Standing next to him at the wheel of the high-end yacht, Radder's best friend, Jack, snapped his fingers to Jimmy Buffett on the radio. They were two versions of one person, really, Radder and Jack, soft software-millionaire nerds, carbon copies of the same bad Ralph Lauren advertisement.

Lounging on the deck behind them, their girlfriends nodded in time to "Margaritaville," swaying slightly in the ocean breeze. They, too, were basically identical—country-club casual, drop-dead gorgeous and dripping diamonds to make Liz Taylor proud.

The upscale yacht barely rippled the water as it cruised around a tiny elevated coral island ringed by magnificent cliffs. Seabirds took to the air all around, their squawks echoing off the vertical rock and endless ocean.

Jack tipped his head back, stared into the almost-too-blue sky. "So I said to him, 'Hey, man, if you're looking for trouble, you came to the right place.'"

He paused.

"And I introduced him to..."

He held up a pudgy fist.

"The convincer. And..."

Held up the other, somehow pudgier, fist.

"The convincer's helper."

Radder giggled like a schoolgirl in appreciation of the lie. Jack checked the Bond girls for their reaction, but they were occupied watching the sunlight flash through their jewelry.

Jack shook his head. He gave Radder an appreciative nod. "Jeez, broheem, you weren't kiddin' about this place."

Radder dug his arm into a nearby mini-fridge and pulled out a wine cooler, a Christmas-morning smile on his already sunburned face. "Like a freakin' National Geographic special, huh?" he asked. "Beautiful. Nothing like it anywhere."

Jack laughed. "Pretty as a hundred-dollar bill...but kinda quiet, you know...spooky quiet."

Radder hummed the theme from *The Twilight Zone*. "Yeah, 'cause we're the only people within a million miles."

As if in direct answer to Radder's claim, his yacht rounded a rock outcropping and was suddenly, terrifyingly, bow to bow with another, larger yacht.

"Shit," Radder screamed. He jammed the boat into reverse and frantically spun the wheel. The trophy girlfriends toppled like tenpins, their cocktail glasses smashing on the deck in an elegant chiming crash.

On the bow of the larger yacht stood a ferocious-looking man, shirtless and completely bald, large gold hoops dangling from both ears. Every inch of his heavily muscled upper body was covered in wild, colorful tattoos. Mr. Clean in a mosh pit.

Jack coughed out a frightened, "What the hell is that?"

Radder slammed the boat into forward gear and full-throttled toward open sea.

Jack's attention locked on the juggernaut behind them. "I-I think they're comin' after us," he said—a shaky whisper that sounded more like a prayer.

Radder looked for all the world as if he might pass out. He gripped the wheel to keep his hands from shaking. "Shitshitshitshit," he mumbled, then stopped suddenly. His eyes widened. He looked over at Jack. "In the cabin, first drawer by the toilet, there's a pistol. Get it."

Jack did his best open-mouthed mannequin impersonation. "A-a pistol?" he stammered. "Like, a gun? What are you doing with—?"

"Just get it!" Radder screamed.

Jack disappeared down the stairs at a heavy run.

The large ship glided smoothly up beside them, powerful engines closing the gap as if the smaller boat was standing still.

In the center of the deck, Tattooed Man stood tall, an apparition in Technicolor, menacing and wild, with a maniacal smile on his face that chilled Radder to the bone, even in the heat of the Archipelago sun. Tattooed Man was surrounded by a dozen other men, all carrying automatic weapons—AK-47 assault rifles and special-forces-issue MK 23 pistols. Heavily armed wolves.

The two now-disheveled pretty young things scrambled back down-boat to Radder.

Tattooed Man gave a signal, and four tubes mounted on the side of his yacht shot grappling hooks and lines onto the deck of the vacationers' yacht. Within seconds, the grappling lines were tight and the two vessels were winched together, side by side. Tattooed Man and the wolf pack hurdled both rails, and Radder found himself within spitting distance of the most frightening group of men he had ever seen.

The women crouched behind Radder, breath heaving as if their credit cards had just been declined at Saks.

Tattooed Man strode forward and stopped, a devilish look on his face. "Cut your engines," he said, his voice deep and raspy, with a thick British accent.

In a trance, Radder cut the engines.

The man gave a slow nod. "Thank you kindly."

Radder tried to raise a trembling hand. "Please," he managed, voice barely audible, "we—"

Tattooed Man lifted his hand, silencing Radder. He put his index finger to his lips. "Shhhhh," he said. "Speak again, and I'll kill you. Then...I'll hurt your feelings." Tattooed Man looked around slowly, playing the silence for maximum effect.

The door to the cabin suddenly burst open with an echoing crash. Radder and the women jumped, all three emitting frightened shrieks. Jack bounded out of the entryway, brandishing an automatic pistol. He waved the pistol back and forth, hands trembling, covering all of the pirates, most of the ocean and a few clouds in the sky.

Tattooed Man and the wolves didn't even turn their heads. It was as if Jack was invisible.

Tattooed Man gave a slight flourish. "My name is Kanna," he said in a grandiose carnival-barker voice. "Or Lord Kanna, if you please."

He lifted his hands high to the horizon.

"I own this ocean."

As Kanna spoke, he moved casually toward Jack, until he was standing directly in front of him. The "convincer" and the "convincer's helper" were shaking so badly at this point that the pistol looked like a maestro's baton.

Kanna shook his head in dramatic sadness. "Careful with that, Your Highness," he offered. "Somebody could get hurt."

Without giving any sign that he was worried at all about the gun pointed at his head, Kanna reached out and casually disarmed Jack. He then grabbed the trembling software millionaire by the shirt collar and gently but firmly dragged him to where the other three were standing.

As he released Jack, Kanna straightened the man's Coke-bottle eyeglasses, then winked at one of the women and blew her a kiss.

He directed his attention to his men. "Go to work," he shouted.

The wolf pack leaped into action, tossing the boat thoroughly and quickly. This was obviously something they had plenty of experience with.

As his enthusiastic crew applied themselves to their craft, Kanna focused on the frightened foursome.

"We're pleased that you've chosen to spend your vacation with us," he said in a friendly tone. "You seem like fine, fine people."

He paused and gave a slight chuckle. "We require a small payment," he continued. "A toll, if you will. A pittance, really, when you consider the skyrocketing costs of piracy nowadays. Cash, jewelry..."

As he spoke, Kanna walked among the vacationers, gently relieving the women of their heavy burden of jewelry. He smiled at them in what he obviously thought was a debonair manner, sparkling white teeth splitting a hideous mask of tattoos. The women appeared to be on the verge of fainting.

Kanna paused, surveying his men's work. "We will not take your food or water...and your credit cards are really of no use to us." He shrugged. "We're strictly cash and carry. Besides, we want you to have some way of immediately replacing the pretty little trinkets we are liberating today."

One of the pirates gave Kanna a signal. Within seconds, all but one of them were back on their own deck, full bags of plunder in hand. The remaining pirate walked up and stood beside Kanna, holding a small plastic-wrapped bundle.

"In exchange for your generous contribution," Kanna said, "we provide you with our unconditional protection."

The last pirate stepped forward and handed the bundle to Radder. Radder accepted it, hands shaking.

"In ancient times," Kanna went on, warming to his speech, "a Roman citizen could walk the length of the emperor's world without fear of attack. Such was the power of Caesar."

He indicated the bundle.

"This is my flag," he said. "If you fly this flag in these waters, you will be completely safe. No one will bother you. No one. Such is my power. So you see, there's really no reason to cut your vacation short."

He spread his arms wide, flexing his rainbow-colored biceps for emphasis. "Enjoy my ocean. It's for the beautiful people...like you and me."

With that, Kanna spun on his heel and strode away. The last of his men followed him. The grappling lines went slack.

Kanna turned and pointed at one of the women. "Do you want to come with me, darlin'?" he asked. "I saw you watchin' me..."

The woman gasped and shrank back. Jack reflexively, almost accidentally, put his arms around her.

Kanna stared, completely deadpan, at his remaining man for a second or two, then they both burst out laughing and leaped to their own deck.

Kanna turned back to the vacationers. "Fly the flag," he shouted.

The pirate engines roared to life. The larger yacht churned the waters, pulling away quickly and disappearing around the curve of the island.

On Radder's yacht, the four vacationers stood like zombies—deflated, disheveled country-club zombies.

Radder took the plastic-wrapped flag and hurled it into the cabin. Both women broke down crying and slumped to the deck.

"Sons of bitches," Radder said in a dull monotone. "Sons of bitches."

Jack stared down into the cabin. He started to speak but could only manage a croak the first time. He took a deep breath, cleared his throat and tried again. "H-he said we should...fly the flag. Maybe we should, you know, fly the flag."

Saying this reminded him of where they were. He looked frantically all around, scanning the horizon for more tattooed bogeymen.

Radder shook his head. "Hell with what he said. Sons of bitches."

Jack simply nodded, too numb to argue about the flag. "Let's just get out of here," he said.

Radder started the engines. He balled his shaking hand into a fist, shut his eyes hard. As the shock overwhelmed him, he stumbled back into the captain's chair and sat down heavily, eyes staring blankly forward.

"Sons of bitches," he mumbled, mostly to himself. "Sons of bitches."

CHAPTER TWO

Caleb Tavington breathed in slowly, held the breath for a count of three, and then exhaled into the conditioned air. He allowed himself to relax, taking a slight edge off the vigilance he had maintained for as long as he could remember.

His eyes scanned the room in a slow circle, taking in his surroundings—a luxury hotel suite, filled with expensive antique furniture. In a wall mirror, he caught sight of himself, lounging in the king-sized Victorian bed. Average height and build, clean-cut hair, now tousled. Dark eyes. Long-sleeve silk pajamas, with the hotel monogram prominently displayed on the chest pocket.

A magnificent floor-to-ceiling aquarium filled the entire far wall of the suite. Caleb's eyes settled on a dazzling array of tropical fish drifting along in the artificial current. Every now and then, an errant wanderer would break free from the routine and swim to the front glass, facing outward toward the mahogany in-room bar. Caleb followed these adventurers with interest, but after a few moments of freedom, each one eventually returned to the safety of his group.

The French doors to the balcony opened and Emma Wallace entered, beautiful in the morning sunlight. She moved to the bed and sat down without a word. Her hand reached over, caressed Caleb's face. He smiled in response.

"It's so beautiful here," she said. "We could stay...couldn't we? Just for a little while longer?"

Caleb laughed, but there was a soft tone of regret in the laugh. "We could," he answered in a voice that carried a slight English accent. "But it would rain, Emma. Eventually it would rain... and we'd get wet."

Emma gave a sad smile, stared down at the bed for a few moments. "I love you, Caleb Tavington," she said, and there was a weight to her voice that dragged on the words. "I've loved you since I was fifteen years old."

She ran her hand through his hair and added, mimicking a man's deep Scottish brogue, "Caleb Tavington is Sean Connery. He's Steve Goddamn McQueen...and you're not."

Caleb raised an eyebrow. "Who said that?"

"Father. To Michael."

"God's blood," Caleb said, shaking his head. "Michael."

Emma cupped Caleb's face in her hands. "How could anyone," she asked, "hate this beautiful face so much?"

"Emma, I made a promise to you and I—"

"You are who you are...and I would be a fool to think that it will be as simple as keeping a promise."

Caleb sat up and drew Emma toward him until their foreheads were touching. The sleeve on his arm slipped back, revealing tattoos on his wrist.

Emma closed her eyes. "I'm afraid, Caleb," she said, her voice breaking.

"It's alright," Caleb said. "Of monsters...people should be afraid."

"The sea that binds us...," Emma whispered.

Caleb gave a quick shake of his head. "No. Not this time. I promise."

Emma opened her eyes, and there were tears in them. "Would it be so bad if we stayed just a little while longer?" she asked. "It's so beautiful..."

A hardness settled in Caleb's eyes, and when he answered, his voice was flat. His eyes returned to the aquarium, restless, as if searching for another wanderer to break free of the routine, free of their lives.

"It would be," he answered, "the most beautiful prison anyone ever served time in."

• • • •

"If they could only see you now."

Emma smiled as she spoke, her voice falling into a natural rhythm, matching the soft blues melody playing in the background. She and Caleb relaxed at a window table in the elegant hotel restaurant. The dining room was deserted, save for the two of them, three nearby waiters and a pianist at the magnificent grand piano.

Caleb nodded to one of the waiters. The man immediately drew the blinds on the windows, darkening the room. Another waiter appeared beside the table, placed two silver candlesticks and lit them.

"They wouldn't know what to make of me," Caleb responded.

One of the waiters refilled Emma's glass from a champagne bottle chilling beside the table. She nodded in thanks, waited until the man stepped away, and then placed a photograph on the table in front of Caleb.

The picture showed four laughing children, three boys and a girl, the boys armed with water pistols, sitting in a floating kayak. Caleb reached out and picked up the picture.

"I've never seen this before," he said.

"My mother took it," Emma explained. "It was her favorite. She said it reminded her of what the future could be."

Caleb nodded. "Good-looking bunch of troublemakers."

"Well, you always were the prettiest boy in the Archipelago," she said with a slight smile. "And we followed you into whatever mischief you could dream up." Her eyes fell onto the picture and lingered there. "I want you to have it," she said.

Caleb considered the offer for a long moment. Finally, he shook his head. "No, Em," he responded. "You should keep it." He pushed the photograph back across the table toward her. "Let it remind *you* of what the future could be."

. . . .

At the restaurant's front entrance, a young couple approached the maître d' desk. Before they began speaking, however, the maître d' raised his hand.

"I'm sorry," he said. "We are closed."

The maître d's eyes flickered to a man standing nearby—Asian in appearance, earnestly smoking a cigarette. The man seemed normal enough, casual in his disposition and demeanor, but there was something threatening about him, some promise of violent things just beneath the surface. The Asian man's eyes moved constantly, scanning every shadowy corner and passerby.

The young man tilted his head in consternation, stared in through the restaurant entry and glared at the maître d'. He pointed out Caleb and Emma, relaxing at their table in an otherwise empty dining room.

"What about them?" the young man asked.

The maître d' didn't even turn his head to look. "I see no one," he responded. "Please, try back at dinner."

The couple stood, dumbfounded, for a full five seconds, and the young man appeared ready to argue, but at that moment, the Asian gentleman took a step forward and fixed his cold, hard stare on the young man's face. All the bluster that the young man had obviously been preparing to unleash on the maître d' disappeared into thin air. He grasped his companion's hand, as if for moral support, then turned away, completely unnerved. The couple hurried off, without even a single glance back.

The Asian man gave the maître d' a nod, then returned to his position against the glass.

· · · ·

From inside the restaurant, Caleb watched the young couple retreat until they were lost from his view. The Asian man glanced in, met Caleb's stare with a nod.

"I see Masu is making friends," Emma said.

Caleb nodded. "Sorry."

Emma smiled in response. There was only understanding on her face. The life that she lived was not a surprise to her.

The piano played softly in the background.

She reached out her hand and placed it on Caleb's. "Everything feels so fragile, love. So...breakable. I—"

"Shhh," Caleb interrupted her, a gentle encouragement. "Don't." He smiled suddenly. "Tell me again what you want," he said.

Emma looked away, biting her lip. Her eyes filled with tears.

"Come on," he pleaded. "Tell me."

Emma laughed through her tears. She took a few moments to compose herself.

"I want an apartment," she said. "A studio apartment, so small that every time we turn around we touch each other. And I want to walk, hand in hand with you, through a crowded Trafalgar Square. Every day. And I want it not to matter who sees us."

"That's a lot of walking," Caleb said.

"And I want to eat in restaurants…"

Caleb looked around, eyebrow raised questioningly.

Emma smiled and continued, "Brightly lit restaurants, with other diners. And I want to dance, Caleb, without caring who's around, all night long if we choose to, because we know we're safe."

Caleb pushed his chair back and stood, offering her his hand. "Well," he said, "I can't give you 'other diners' right now, but I would dearly love a dance"—he gave the room a dramatic once-over, his eyes scanning all of the nearby tables—"with the most beautiful woman in the room."

Emma took his hand and stood. She rested her head on Caleb's shoulder and they danced, slowly, beside their table. "And I want to cook you breakfast," Emma murmured. "How is it possible that I've never cooked for you?"

They continued on, swaying gently to the sad sounds coming from the piano.

"Do you promise it, Caleb?"

"All of it," Caleb responded. "On my honor. I promise all of it."

Emma nodded, closed her eyes. "And you?" she said. "I've never asked you. What do you want?"

Caleb considered the question for a long moment before finally answering.

"I want to wake up one morning and see the gray in your hair," he said. "I want to see laugh lines around your eyes and kiss your beautiful wrinkled face…because it will mean that we've been able to grow old together."

Emma smiled, tears flowing down her face. "If they could only see you now," she whispered.

• • • •

An ocean away from the soft sounds of a grand piano and a couple dancing alone in romantic lighting, the conference room on the Wallace family yacht was dark, the windows shuttered. The only light was a single dim lamp in one corner. Luxurious and well appointed, the room was fitted in a classic old-world design, harkening back to the British Colonial history of the Wallace family themselves.

Eamon "Black" Wallace sat at the mahogany conference table, a scowl on his face, watching the smoke from his cigar curl toward the ceiling. Eamon was a large man, built for hurting people, his bearded face lined and hard from years of harsh living. There was nothing soft about Black Wallace.

Also seated at the conference table was Black's second-in-command, Tanner. Tanner looked the veteran roughneck that he was, but, somehow, next to Black, he came off about as intimidating as a choirboy.

Black directed his gaze at a line of photographs on the conference table in front of him, pictures of Caleb Tavington and Emma Wallace having brunch together at an upscale hotel restaurant.

He smoked his cigar slowly, his face a mask of hatred and anger. "It's time, Tanner," he said, in a voice thick with rage. "Time to change the world."

Tanner nodded, but his eyes were wary. "If you're sure," he said, "then we're ready. But I don't have to tell you, Eamon, the Archipelago's not a forgiving place. So be sure."

Black exhaled a thick cloud of smoke, then used his cigar to burn a hole through Caleb's face in one of the photographs. "Some things must not be allowed," he growled. "Some things cry out…for the remedy of eternity."

"Still," Tanner offered, carefully, "I—"

"They take, Tanner," Black interrupted. "It's what they do. It's what they've done for generations. They'll suck the very marrow from your bones." He looked down at the pictures again. "They'll eat your children. It must end."

Tanner nodded seriously, watching Black Wallace like a baby springbok in the presence of a lounging lion. A soft knock sounded at the door.

Tanner glanced over. "They're ready," he said.

Both men stood. Black led the way out of the room and up a flight of wooden stairs.

At the top of the stairs, they stepped through an exterior door and onto the deck of the Wallace yacht, shading their eyes against the bright sunshine. In the brilliant yellow light, Black presented a fierce picture, intense eyes sweeping back and forth like a wild animal trapped in a cage.

The deck of the yacht was crowded—rough-cut men and a few women standing shoulder to shoulder, several deep. At the front of the crowd, a woman knelt, crying, clutching an infant with one arm and a sobbing young boy with the other.

The focus of the crowd's attention was a prisoner, kneeling in the foredeck, his hands bound behind his back. The man's face was puffy with old and new bruises, lips freshly split and bleeding. Next to the chained man stood his executioner, shirtless and tattooed, pistol held casually at his side. The executioner seemed perfectly at ease, even bored by the proceedings. Killing the man kneeling at his feet was obviously not something he was going to lose any sleep over.

Black surveyed the scene, his gaze moving slowly along the deck, then past it. The Wallace yacht lay anchored in the center of a small bay twenty yards from shore. On the beach, a second crowd of people stood quietly, watching.

Movement above him on the yacht's bridge drew his attention.

His son, Michael, stood at the window, staring down, an almost sorrowful expression on his face.

Tanner followed Black's gaze. As he looked up, Michael turned and moved away from the glass.

Black Wallace snorted in disgust, shot a hard look at Tanner and shook his head.

"The universe has conspired against me, Tanner," he said. "My son cannot stand the sight of blood. Alistair Tavington's son, on the other hand, drinks blood. When I need strength and loyalty most, I am met with"—he glanced back up at the bridge—"weakness and"—he looked over at the chained man—"betrayal."

Black smoldered, eyes set deep in his face.

He turned to address the gathered crowd. As he lifted his hand, a complete silence dropped on the deck like a smothering blanket. Not a single sound could be heard.

"What you see here is a tragedy," he announced in a voice that carried across the water all the way to the shore. "A man without honor, and thus...without value."

Tanner stepped forward and emptied the contents of a small leather pouch at the bound man's feet. A handful of jeweled necklaces and precious rings clattered onto the deck.

"This ocean," Black continued, his voice rising in increased anger, "and all that is in it, is mine. No man can steal what belongs to the Wallace family."

Tanner nodded to the executioner, who raised his pistol.

The young boy twisted away from his mother and scrambled, wailing, to the kneeling man. He threw his arms around the man's bruised and broken face, blocking the pistol barrel.

The executioner tried to pull the boy away with one hand while angling for a clean shot with the other, but the boy twisted and turned frantically, refusing to relinquish his hold.

The boy's mother started forward, but a nearby man stopped her. Unable to get clear, the mother was forced to watch, her face twisted in terror, as her son struggled desperately to protect his father.

There were now some smiles in the crowd, enjoyment of the executioner's frustration. Finally, unable to get a good shot, the executioner stepped back, looked over at Tanner and shrugged.

Tanner smiled at the executioner's embarrassment and simply watched in amusement.

Tears streamed down the face of the bound man. He whispered softly to his son, but the boy shook his head fiercely and gripped his father more tightly, sobs racking his body.

Black Wallace had seen enough. "Shoot the boy as well," he said, his voice flat.

Tanner barked out a laugh, then stopped short at the look on Black's face. "You can't be serious," he said in disbelief. "He's just a child, Eamon."

"Children grow up to be heroes, Tanner." Black's voice was as cold as ice. "Shoot the boy," he repeated.

Tanner did not give the order. He stared at the kneeling man, then looked over at the woman and motioned her forward to retrieve her son. The roughneck holding her immediately released her.

The boy saw his mother coming and started shrieking, rending the air with his screams of anguish.

"For God's sake." Black spat the words out and strode forward.

The crowd fell silent.

A blade flashed in Black's hand.

Black reached the kneeling man at the same time the woman did. She threw herself on her son, protecting the infant in her arms and breaking the older boy's hold on his father, forcing the boy to the deck. She covered her son's wriggling body with her own.

Black grabbed the bound man by the throat and pulled him roughly to his feet. With two powerful thrusts, Black's heavy blade slashed across the back of the man's legs, tearing through fabric, skin and sinew, hamstringing the man.

Blood splashed onto the woman and her son. The man screamed in pain as his legs twitched and went limp.

Black casually dragged the whimpering man to the open gangplank door, leaving a greasy river of blood on the deck.

He hurled the man off the deck and into the ocean, the man's legs flopping uselessly in the air. The man hit the water, thrashed wildly in a pink froth, then sank. Within seconds, bubbles breaking the surface were the only clue as to what had just happened.

Black turned and glared at the crowd on deck, now subdued by the sudden brutality. His eyes flashed with a terrible anger, mouth twisted in a snarl. No one moved. The only sound was the muffled screaming of the boy under his mother.

Black turned and stalked off the deck, a malevolent shadow, leaving a trail of darkness in his wake.

CHAPTER THREE

The cacophony rising from the commercial boat dock was like constant multipitched thunder. Engines and animals, diesel-powered loaders and cranes, all mixed together in a symphony of frenetic sound. Grinding, squawking and roaring combined with dozens of languages shouted at the top of workmen lungs.

The blistering Southeast Asian sun baked everything under it. Steam rose from sizzling asphalt and the freshly hosed decks of every type of ship, commercial or otherwise. The entire waterfront was a madhouse of people and cargo and noise.

From the gates of the dock area, a limousine worked its way slowly toward the water, finally stopping in the shadow of the largest pleasure yacht tied to the main receiving pier. One of the passenger doors opened and Caleb stepped out, duffel bag in hand. Immediately, Masu was beside him, eyes moving—searching out the shadows.

Above them, aboard the yacht, Samuel Tavington, Caleb's brother, walked out onto the deck. Samuel was in his twenties, a slighter, softer version of his brother. The younger Tavington smiled and lifted his arm in an exaggerated wave.

"Caleb," he shouted over the din of the loading dock.

Caleb smiled up at his brother. Samuel bounded down the gangplank and the two men embraced.

"God, Caleb," Samuel said, an ear-to-ear smile on his face. "It's so good to see you. It feels like forever."

Caleb laughed. "It really has," he responded. "We've all missed you very much, Sam."

Caleb took a step back, held his arm out and turned to Masu. "Look at him, Masu, the boy comes back a man."

Masu offered a noncommittal nod.

Samuel watched Masu for a moment, as if he was expecting something more. Realizing that nothing more was coming, he stepped forward.

"Let me take your bag, Caleb. Our rented palace awaits."

Samuel picked up Caleb's duffel and slung it over his shoulder.

"How long do we have it for?" Caleb asked, eyeing the vessel.

"Seven days," Samuel responded.

Caleb nodded, and the three men walked together up the gangplank.

· · · ·

As the Archipelago sun pushed its way high into the center of the sky, the Tavington rented yacht cut across the glassy ocean at speed. In the main lounge, Caleb sipped his drink, standing near the doorway of the yacht's dining room, watching Samuel over the rim of his glass. Both men were dressed smartly for the noon meal, all the way down to bow ties and shoes polished to a glistening luster. Caleb smiled. Samuel seemed perfectly suited to the picture, a young aristocrat seated in an elegant room, surrounded by crystal and china, with soft classical music playing in the background. Right out of a Jane Austen novel. Samuel met Caleb's eyes and grinned, as if he could tell what his older brother was thinking.

Movement outside a large porthole window drew Caleb's attention, and he stepped forward. An Indonesian Coast Guard cutter near the horizon was towing a sleek, powerful-looking speedboat—an impressive craft that made the Coast Guard cutter look small and old by comparison.

Masu moved quietly to Caleb's side, watching the cutter and the speed boat.

"Nice boat," Caleb said.

Masu nodded and lit a cigarette. Caleb stood for a few moments, watching the scene very carefully. It was as if he wanted to remember every detail.

A small bell chimed, indicating lunch was ready.

Samuel stood, eyes on Caleb. "Everything alright?" he asked.

Caleb nodded. "Masu and I are just admiring a very expensive boat, flying interesting colors."

Samuel started toward the window, but Caleb turned back toward the room.

"Oh well," Caleb said. "Let's eat."

• • • •

Later, Caleb and Samuel relaxed over the remains of their lunch, enjoying Tchaikovsky's 1812 Overture on the sound system.

Masu entered. Before he could even step out of the doorway, however, the yacht's cook bumbled into the room and shouldered Masu aside. He was a fat man, and sweaty, face contorted in fear, his breath coming in heaving, jiggling gasps.

"S-s-sir," he blurted, panic-stricken. "We have trouble, sir. Big trouble, sir. Pirates." He stumbled to a halt, looking as if he could collapse at any moment.

Caleb raised an eyebrow. "Pirates? Are you sure?"

The cook, still gasping for breath, replied with an emphatic nod.

Caleb stood, reached into his back waistband and pulled out a revolver. Without any visible signs of worry, he checked the cylinder, then tucked the weapon away again.

He turned to Samuel. "Stay here," he said. "I'll check it out."

He motioned that Masu should lead the way and then followed him out the door.

Masu emerged on deck, moving slowly, almost lethargically. Caleb followed, with the cook blubbering and sniffling behind him.

On the far end of the deck stood Kanna, hideously magnificent in the afternoon sunlight, his tattoos a dazzling array of color and design. His pirate yacht sat tethered not two yards away across open water, so close that its silhouette framed Kanna as if he was posing for a picture. Fifteen shirtless men stood tall in the bow of the ship.

Kanna raised his hands to the sky, milking the theatre of the moment. "Do you have American chocolate on board?" he shouted. "I love American chocolate."

He walked slowly toward Caleb, playing every moment for dramatic purpose, surveying the beautiful yacht as he went.

Behind Caleb, the cook started to sob.

"Snickers, mainly," Kanna continued, almost to himself. "Hershey's, M&Ms..."

Caleb turned to Masu. "We do have some American chocolate on board. Don't we, Masu?"

Masu didn't respond. He remained completely still, eyes on Kanna.

Caleb directed his attention back to Kanna. "However," he said, "judging by the look of that stomach, perhaps a nice green salad would be better."

Caleb's remark was greeted by complete silence on deck. Behind him, the cook fainted dead away, his body crumpling to the deck in an extended thud.

Kanna stopped short, as if he had walked into a wall, a look of sincere pain on his face. He turned back to his men, who leaned forward expectantly, their eyes shiny and eager.

Suddenly, Kanna burst out in thunderous laughter, head thrown back to the sky. The pirates behind him joined in.

Caleb smiled and strode toward the tattooed giant of a man.

Before Caleb could close the distance, Kanna leaped forward and enveloped him in a mighty bear hug, lifting him clear off the deck.

Caleb laughed and did his best to return the hug, to almost no avail. He was simply forced to endure the constricting tattooed squeeze.

Finally, Kanna put him down and gave him a thorough once-over, a wide grin on his multicolored face. "Bloody hell," he said. "You look good, Caleb. You should take a vacation more often."

Caleb put his hand on Kanna's shoulder, his face suddenly serious. "The sea that binds us," he said in a respectful voice.

Kanna nodded, acknowledging the change in tone. When he answered, his voice was more formal. "The sea that binds us," he said.

Kanna's men stood at attention, silent and unmoving. Caleb let his gaze wash over them.

"Passo," Caleb said. One of the pirates tilted his head back. "Get my things and transfer them to the ship."

Caleb turned to Kanna and gave him a short nod. Kanna immediately started barking orders. The men flew into action. In the midst of the activity, Caleb walked to the far rail and hurdled it, landing in a tidy three-point stance on the pirate ship.

Back on the luxury yacht, Samuel emerged onto the deck.

A shrill whistle from one of the men alerted Kanna to Samuel's presence. He looked over and roared with laughter, his smile as wide as his face.

"Sammy," he shouted, scrambling across the deck until he was standing in front of the younger Tavington.

"Good to see you, boy," he said. He took a step back and gave Samuel a good look. "Christ, you're prettier than Caleb now."

Samuel seemed a little unsure of how he should respond. His eyes flickered to all of the movement around him, all of the rough-cut men in determined motion, before he finally came back to Kanna.

He cleared his throat and held out his hand. "The sea that binds—" he began.

Kanna knocked Samuel's hand aside. "Hell with that," he bellowed and caught Samuel up in a smothering hug, lifting him up just as he had done Caleb.

Samuel coughed out a constricted laugh. Kanna shook him up and down a few times, then once to the side for good measure. Finally, he returned him to the deck.

"It's good to see you again, Kanna," Samuel said with a shy grin. "I've missed you."

Kanna clapped him on the shoulder. "Go get on the boat, boyo," he ordered. "I'll take care of your delicates."

Samuel nodded and gave Kanna a salute. "Aye-aye, Admiral," he responded and started toward the far rail.

Kanna watched him go. He waited until Samuel had safely leaped the distance to the other boat before turning away. As he did, Masu walked past, heading to the far end of the deck.

Kanna grimaced in dramatic fashion. "Surprised somebody hasn't killed you yet, sunshine," he said.

"Yes," Masu responded, in perfect English and without so much as turning his head. "So am I."

Kanna laughed.

Masu allowed the barest hint of a smile to cross his face, then he was at the far rail and onto the adjacent ship.

CHAPTER FOUR

Caleb rubbed his eyes as he flipped through a sheaf of papers on a table in front of him.

"Everything looks fine, Kanna," he said. "I expected no different."

Caleb, Samuel, Kanna and Masu were all seated in an elegant onboard lounge, dressed for an early dinner. Papers and ledgers covered the surfaces of three tables arranged around them, along with several wine bottles, crystal goblets and half-eaten meals on china plates.

An Indonesian servant in a crisp white coat circled the room, cleaning up. Several other servants stood nearby, at attention.

Kanna made a slight flourish, a half-bow from his seated position. "Well, thank you, kind and pretty master."

Samuel giggled. Caleb turned toward him. "Sam," he asked, "did you follow all that?"

"Yeah," Samuel answered with a nod. "Pretty straightforward stuff."

"Good," Caleb said. "Could you run these books if you had to?"

Kanna leaned back in his chair. He gave Caleb a questioning look, which Caleb ignored.

"Run the books?" Kanna snorted. "S'truth, the boy just finished four grueling years at Harvard." He winked at Samuel. "You want his head to explode?"

Caleb kept his eyes on Samuel. "Sam?" he repeated.

Samuel paused for a moment, understanding that Caleb was asking a real question. A serious question. "I think so," he answered.

Caleb let his eyes stay on Samuel for a moment longer, and nobody in the room was inclined to hurry him at this point. Finally, he nodded. "Good."

At that moment, a knock sounded at the door.

"Come," Caleb said.

The door opened slowly, and Passo stepped in. He bowed, with obvious respect for the room. "Rebel ship," he said. "One hundred yards off starboard."

Caleb and the others immediately stood, straightening their dinner jackets and ties. They followed Passo out of the dining lounge and up to the main deck.

Once on deck, Caleb, Samuel and Kanna moved to the forward rail in a tight line, facing the approaching rebel ship. On the rebel deck, two men in dress uniform stood at the rail.

Caleb focused on the two rebel officers. "I don't see a captain," he said.

Kanna's eyes hardened. As the two ships passed each other, a man in captain's stripes joined the two rebels on deck. He stood for only a moment, then turned his back quickly and walked away.

Caleb stared after the ship as it passed, his jaw clenched. "What was that?" he asked, his voice low. "Does he want me to go after him...burn his ship down to the waterline?"

Kanna paused a moment before answering, choosing his words with care. "He'll say it was a legitimate pass-by, Caleb. He was on deck, after all."

Caleb fixed Kanna with a hard glare and said, "What the hell is going on?"

"Money, boyo," Kanna answered. "Per usual. They want pain and sufferin' money."

"They've always wanted more. Why the insult now?"

Kanna shook his head, as much at a loss as Caleb. "It's a sorry bloody day," he said, "when beggars aspire to be choosers."

• • • •

Later, Kanna stood close to the window on the ship's bridge, binoculars pressed to his face. He handed the binoculars to Caleb. In the near distance, plumes of black smoke billowed from a yacht on fire. At the moment, the vessel was being looted by a motley group of Indonesian pirates. Caleb used the binoculars to scan the burning ship, the pirates on board, and the ship drifting next to it.

Caleb handed the binoculars back to an angry Kanna. "What's the problem?" he asked.

"That yacht," Kanna said. "We bounced it already. It's ours."

Caleb shook his head, a look of disbelief in his eyes. "Jesus, Kanna. Has everyone gone insane?"

He increased the ship's speed, then gave control of the wheel to Passo, who had just entered the bridge. Soon, Caleb and all of the men on board, save Passo, were standing on the main deck, armed to the teeth.

Passo eased the ship expertly up to the burned-out vacationers' yacht that Kanna had looted only days before. Two of Caleb's men stepped into shipside turrets and strapped themselves to a pair of .50-caliber mounted deck guns. The triple-barreled rotary machine guns were protected behind four inches of steel and a vision plate of bulletproof glass, reinforced by mesh. Both men wore safety goggles and Kevlar vests. In a close-up firefight, the .50s were capable of wreaking immense damage, to the tune of two thousand heavy-jacketed rounds per minute.

The .50-cal guns swiveled to line up their sights, one on the ruined yacht, and one on the pirate ship.

For their part, the Indonesian pirates had stopped their dirty work and were all standing still, eyes on Caleb and his men. Many nervous glances were also directed toward the .50-cal heavy machine guns pointed directly at them. They were a ragtag bunch, dirty and unkempt, sporting a collection of mismatched weapons, some obviously homemade. Bottom-feeders.

On the vacationers' yacht deck, the body of Radder was sprawled out, bullet-ridden. Nearby, another body lay smashed against the side rail, blood pooling all around it. The once-beautiful deck was pockmarked and ruined, splintered wood and broken glass scattered everywhere.

Passo reduced engine speed, idling the ship directly beside the vacationers' yacht. Caleb and his men leaped to the deck, and Caleb's men immediately began rounding up the Indo pirates, who, though armed and obviously dangerous, did not resist at all.

The leader of the Indo pirates stepped forward, hands extended, palms up. Beady eyes, greasy hair—Iggy Pop with a gun. There was blood on his arms, from wrists to elbows, and a good deal of it splashed on his shirt and face. He stood there like a statue, arms held out in front of him, waiting to be told what to do.

Caleb focused on the man. "What is your name?" he asked. At the sound of his voice, even the whispering and shuffling among the Indo pirates stopped.

The Indo leader cleared his throat. "Copsa. Sir," he answered in thickly accented English.

Caleb allowed his gaze to sweep across the deck, lingering here and there on individual pirates. He turned to Kanna with a questioning look. Kanna shook his head.

"Copsa," Caleb said. "Where is our flag?"

Copsa's face registered his confusion. He tilted his head, as if he wasn't sure about the question. "There was no flag. Sir."

Kanna stepped forward, face like stone. "Liar," he said.

Copsa shot a worried glance back at one of his men. The man shook his head sharply, an emphatic no.

Copsa turned back to Caleb. "There was no flag, sir," he insisted, with careful respect. "It is the truth."

Caleb took a few paces forward, until he was standing directly in front of Copsa. He leaned in so that their faces were only inches apart. "Copsa," he asked, his voice low. "Do you know who I am?"

Copsa swallowed hard. He nodded. "You are God," he answered.

Caleb allowed this response to hang in the air for a moment. All around him, the silence stretched on.

"If you put our colors in the water," he said, and the words echoed in the stillness like the clanging chimes of doom, "I will see that it takes you a week to die."

Caleb turned to his men. "Toss it."

The words were like a match to gasoline, and his crew jumped into action. They were a whirlwind, efficient and quick, searching the boat top to bottom in less time than it would take a normal person to simply walk through it.

Caleb and Kanna stood in the open sunshine, holding the Indonesian pirates in stasis just by the weight of their presence.

A yell sounded from the below-deck cabin.

Caleb moved to the stairway and descended, Kanna close behind. At the bottom, he stepped into a stately cabin—well-appointed suite, multiple rooms and adjoining living spaces. The vacationers' yacht was every bit a luxury vessel, high-end touches all the way down to the smallest detail.

At the moment, the below-deck suite was a disaster, broken and ransacked, as if a malevolent hurricane had roared through it. Everything had been smashed, upended or torn.

At the far end of the cabin, one of Caleb's men held up a plastic-wrapped bundle. The flag, undisturbed in its original packaging.

Behind Caleb, Kanna let out a long sigh. "Fools," he said. "They didn't fly it."

Caleb nodded. He scanned the room slowly, eyes lingering on separate piles of debris.

As he finished his visual sweep, he noticed one of the sleeping berth doors was ajar, and what appeared to be a human foot visible in the opening. He stepped forward and pushed the door.

In the sleeping berth, both of the vacationing women were lying dead in the single queen bed, both naked, gagged and covered with blood. They had obviously been savagely beaten and abused.

Caleb stared at the horrific scene for a long moment, taking it all in as his face hardened.

He turned and started toward the stairs. Kanna intercepted him before he reached them. "You can't change the world, boyo," he said in a voice low enough that only Caleb could hear. "These animals stink, I agree. But they're abiding by the rules we created. They're our stinking animals."

Caleb stopped short, his path blocked by Kanna, his face livid. "Maybe the old rules aren't enough anymore," he said.

Kanna nodded. "Maybe," he agreed, "and if you say it's time to flip the script, then I'm lock, stock and barrel with you. But the old rules work, Caleb, and it'd be a shit trying to teach these monkeys manners."

Kanna made no move to clear Caleb's path.

Caleb took a deep breath. Then another. And another.

Kanna watched until he was sure that Caleb was operating on an even keel again. Finally, he stepped aside.

Caleb walked slowly up the stairs.

Once on deck, he continued on without slowing, walking straight toward the far rail, looking neither left or right, ignoring everything but what was directly in front of him.

The Indonesian pirates stood quietly, like defendants awaiting the verdict. As Caleb walked by, Copsa raised his arms in a questioning shrug and started toward him, but one of Caleb's men jammed the butt of a rifle into Copsa's chest and pushed him back roughly.

At the end of the deck, Caleb was just about to hurdle the rail when he saw a torn, bloodied pair of women's underwear lying near the sidewall. He stopped suddenly—and so did every single person on deck. It was as if the entire world held its breath.

Caleb spun around, his face set in a mask of anger. He strode aggressively back toward Copsa.

Realizing that the situation had now disintegrated, Copsa reached into his sash. Caleb's men raised their rifles, ready to open fire.

"Leave him," Caleb ordered with a snarl.

Copsa drew out a long, jagged knife, but before he could even drop into a fighting stance, Caleb was on him, lightning-quick with a spinning back fist to Copsa's temple.

The knife skittered harmlessly across the deck.

As Copsa staggered back, Caleb drove into him with a combination of powerful punches to the man's face and abdomen. Copsa crumpled to the deck. Caleb slammed his knee down onto Copsa's chest and began a clinical, vicious beating.

The assembled men watched for a full thirty seconds, until Kanna finally stepped forward and put his arm on Caleb's shoulder.

Caleb stopped, his breath heaving, blood spattered all over his face and the front of his shirt. He stood, wiping his mouth with the back of his hand. Beneath him, Copsa was a broken, bloody mess.

Once on his feet again, Caleb tilted his head back and stared down the Indonesian pirates, his eyes wild and cloudy. Not one of them could meet his stare.

Kanna signaled the Tavington men, giving an extra nod to the two strapped into the .50-cal guns.

Caleb noticed the signal. "No," he said, shaking his head.

Kanna grimaced. "We have to, now."

"No," Caleb repeated. "These men go free."

"Caleb..."

"They go free, Kanna."

Caleb surveyed the Indonesian pirates gathered on the deck. Once he was sure he had every man's attention, he spoke.

"This is my ocean," he said in a voice that offered no room for compromise. "Don't come back. Not ever."

Kanna leaned in close. "The thing about rats, Caleb," he said. "They're forgetful."

But Caleb was already starting toward the Tavington ship. "Let them keep what they took from this yacht, Kanna," he called back over his shoulder. "And cut them loose."

Kanna snorted in frustration. He scanned the Indonesian pirates and made a face of disdain, as if he was looking at something on the bottom of his shoe. Finally, he barked out an order.

Caleb hurdled the rail back onto his own ship, where Samuel was standing. Samuel's eyes were on the sprawled and bloody form of Copsa. Caleb gave a short nod to Samuel and walked past him and down the stairs to below deck.

Kanna wandered over to the rail of the vacationers' yacht and stood for a moment, only a few yards across open water from Samuel. He shook his head.

"Sammy boy," he said. "Your brother just threw away two hundred years of tradition in thirty seconds."

Kanna leaned over and spat into the water, then looked back at Sammy as a devilish grin spread over his face.

"Goddamn," he added. "It's good to have him back."

Caleb's men were off the vacationers' yacht and back onto their own ship within two minutes. Passo, still at the wheel, reversed in a crisp arc, then full-throttled out to open sea.

The Indonesian pirates watched in hate-filled silence as the Tavington yacht motored away.

CHAPTER FIVE

In the bridge of the Tavington yacht, Caleb assembled a patchwork mosaic of maps on a table in front of him, working the line of a protractor between a series of islands. Across the table sat Kanna, pretending to pay close attention to what Caleb was doing but fiddling with a whetstone and blade. Finally he yawned, giving up the charade, and simply leaned back in his chair, eyes closed. The Archipelago sun had baked most of the day away, but the heat was still dancing along the ship's deck in shimmery waves.

Passo stood at the bridge window, watching the approach of a freighter in the near distance. It was a massive ship, plowing through the ocean, leaving a tree-sized wake as it came.

Samuel entered, his face red and already a little sunburned. "Ship on the bow," he said.

"Marchana freighter, Caleb," Passo added. "The *St. Christopher.*"

Caleb sat back in his seat with a sigh. Kanna shook himself to wakefulness. As he did, he caught Caleb's eye and grimaced. "Damn," he said.

Samuel looked over with a frown. "Damn? What do you mean, damn?" His voice brightened as he spoke. "The *St. Christopher* is Zoo's ship, isn't it?"

"That's right, Sammy boy," Kanna answered in a voice that was suddenly uncharacteristically solemn. "It's still Zoo's ship."

Sammy clapped his hands, delighted, a big boyish grin spreading across his face. "Yeah," he enthused, "I was hoping to see him. Good old Zoo."

"Go put a coat on, Sam," Caleb said.

Kanna chewed on the inside of his lip, obviously mulling something over in his mind. He leaned forward toward Caleb. "Maybe Sammy should mind the fort, Caleb," he offered carefully.

"What?" Samuel blurted out. "Have you been in the sun too long? No way. I'm going up there. Give me a minute." So saying, he rushed out, slamming the door on his way.

Kanna exhaled, a loud, dramatic sound. "Caleb…"

"Life is hard, Kanna," Caleb interrupted. "For some more than others."

Caleb stood, straightened his coat, and followed Samuel out the door.

Moments later, Caleb, Kanna and Samuel were all on deck, watching the *St. Christopher* slow its approach. In the shadow of the bridge, Masu lounged against the deck rail, cigarette attached to his lip.

Fifty yards in front of them, the *St. Christopher* cut its engines.

"Pay attention, Sam," Caleb instructed.

Masu lifted his head, more alert now. Kanna scanned the Marchana freighter's decks. A man in a white captain's hat appeared out of a stairwell and moved to the bow, where he stood in plain sight. It was the ship's captain, Zoo Cali.

Samuel waved. "There's Zoo," he said with excitement in his voice.

"Give Sam a gun, Masu," Caleb said.

Samuel turned his head sharply. "A gun? For what?"

Masu produced a gun, seemingly out of thin air. He slid forward a step and held it out to Samuel.

"Put it in your back waistband, boyo," Kanna suggested. "Visible weaponry is for the unbathed masses. The common folk." Kanna winked.

Samuel made a point of eyeing the two pistols protruding, cartoonlike, from Kanna's waistband.

"Gotcha, Kanna, but I don't understand why—"

"Sam," Caleb cut Samuel short. "This is not a social call. We're not here to visit Zoo. This is what we do…so pay attention."

Appropriately chastised, Samuel gave Caleb a quick nod. He accepted the pistol from Masu and tucked it into his back waistband.

Kanna stepped closer to Caleb. "You're the king o' the world, Caleb," he whispered, "but are you sure that Sammy—"

Caleb lifted his hand, and Kanna stopped talking. "Do your job," Caleb ordered.

Kanna shrugged and flashed a hand signal.

From out of the shadow of the bridge above, two Tavington pirates stepped forward onto the deck, armed with Japanese-modified Panzerfaust rocket launchers—capable of blowing through thirty inches of steel. They pointed the launchers directly at the *St. Christopher*'s hull, just above the waterline.

Caleb waited until the men were settled before he spoke. "Let's go."

• • • •

Minutes later, Caleb was seated in the *St. Christopher* captain's office, across a well-ordered desk from Zoo Cali, the captain of the freighter. Directly behind Caleb stood Samuel, all smiles, and further back, Kanna. Masu lounged near the door, which was manned by an armed *St. Christopher* guard.

The captain's office was well used but tidy. Chartbooks and ledgers lined cases along every wall. There was nothing out of place, nothing that required cleaning or adjusting. Captain Zoo Cali obviously ran a tight operation.

Zoo slid a thick manila envelope across the desk to Caleb. "Two hundred fifty thousand dollars," he said. "That's my ship, four times this quarter."

Caleb picked up the envelope and handed it back to Kanna, who slid it into his waistband, beside his pistols.

Zoo smiled at Samuel. "And now, Samuel, I have something for you. In honor of your return from school."

He stood and made his way over to a wall cabinet. He graced his audience with a mysterious smile and paused for a moment, drawing out the suspense, then reached behind the cabinet and produced a baseball bat. With a magician's flourish, he handed it to Samuel.

"There you are, Harvard man," he announced with a proud smile. "A little piece of Boston, to remind you. I wasn't sure exactly when you'd be back, so I kept it on board with me."

Samuel took the bat with a grin. He turned it over in his hands, examining it. His eyes widened.

"Zoo...you shouldn't have," he said, and his tone was hushed. He was obviously touched by the gesture. "Signed by Ted Williams? Are you kidding me?"

"In nineteen forty-one," Zoo said. "You know what that means, don't you?"

Samuel gave a loud, appreciative exhale. "Forty-one? The year he hit four hundred?" Samuel shook his head. "Zoo, this must have cost you a fortune."

Zoo waved his hand dismissively. "That's none of your business, my boy," he laughed. "Besides, my accountant will write it off as an operating expense." He winked at Caleb. "And I'll report it stolen. Collect the insurance."

Strangely, Caleb didn't respond to Zoo's jovial banter. His face appeared cast in stone. Kanna took two small steps forward, so that he was standing between Samuel and Zoo.

"We weren't expecting you today, Zoo," Caleb said, his voice low and somber. "Your run isn't scheduled until next week."

Zoo shrugged. "Yes, well, I have a vacation coming. Las Vegas, the Bellagio. You know the Bellagio?"

Caleb shook his head.

"My travel agent says Las Vegas has the best waffles," Zoo went on. "Anyway, I wanted to take a few extra days, so I switched my scheduled run with Captain Boniol, and he'll take next week."

Caleb sighed. "You have no idea how sad that makes me," he said.

At these words, Zoo's smile died.

"I'm sorry it was you," Caleb finished.

Masu stepped quickly forward, took the bat out of Samuel's hand and swung it with shattering force into the face of the guard at the door. The guard crumpled to the floor.

At the same time, Kanna hooked a hard punch into Zoo's belly. Zoo bent forward, gasping in pain. Kanna grabbed him by the hair and forced him to his knees.

Samuel flinched and jumped back, his face twisted in shock. "Kanna," he yelled. "What the hell—"

Caleb's voice cut through Samuel's surprised shout. "Tell me about the *St. Jude*, Zoo," he said.

On the floor, Zoo struggled for breath. He grimaced as Kanna forced him to lift his head and look at Caleb. "The *St. Jude*?" he stammered. "Caleb, I can explain..."

Kanna drew out one of his pistols and jammed it into Zoo's mouth, muffling him and taking out a few pretty porcelains in the process.

Caleb lifted his hand. "No, that's alright," he said. "While you swallow those teeth, let me tell you about the *St. Jude*. It is a Marchana freighter just like this one. Class B hold. Fitted for automobiles, capable of delivering one thousand midsized sedans...and ten days ago it crossed Tavington water without permission. It spent two days in the Archipelago and then slipped out near the China Strait."

Caleb placed both hands on the table and pushed himself to his feet.

"The Tavingtons have waited ten days, Zoo, for the Marchana Line to make it right, to explain why one of your ships enjoyed our protected water and didn't pay us a dime. Ten days is too long."

Caleb nodded to Kanna, who took the gun out of Zoo's now-bloody mouth.

Zoo spat blood out onto the floor. His body shook from fear. "Caleb, please," he begged. "It was a mistake. The captain lost navigation. He didn't know where he was. As soon as he realized he was in your water, he got out...right away. Please, you must believe me."

Caleb produced a pistol from his waistband. "There is nothing I 'must' do, Zoo," he said, shaking his head. "And if it was a mistake, it was a costly one, because it just killed you."

Caleb put the gun against Zoo's forehead.

"Caleb, wait," Samuel pleaded. His face was pale, and like Zoo, his body shook from the shock and fear of the moment. "He's telling the truth. It was an accident."

On the floor, Zoo had begun to cry. "Please, Caleb," he sobbed. "Please."

Caleb turned to Samuel. "If we allow people to have these kinds of accidents, Sam," he said, his voice cold, "then two days unaccounted for will turn into three, three days into a week, and before long we lose control of our own water."

Samuel shook his head. He reached out a trembling hand and placed it gently on Caleb's shoulder.

"It won't happen again, Caleb," he said. He swallowed hard and glanced down at Zoo. "Right, Zoo? It was an accident."

Zoo's voice was barely audible through the tears. "Please, Caleb," he mumbled. "I swear...please..."

Caleb pulled the hammer back on his pistol.

Zoo shut his eyes, tears streaming down his face. He began mouthing a silent prayer.

Samuel squeezed Caleb's shoulder, and he looked on the verge of a breakdown. Tears filled his eyes. "Caleb..."

Caleb hesitated. He cast a long glance at Samuel's anguished face, then shifted his gaze to Zoo's gifted baseball bat, now lying on the floor where Masu had dropped it. Ted Williams. 1941. The sprawling signature and etched-in date were smeared with blood.

Finally, Caleb exhaled, a slow, feathery sound. The whisper of it was so strangely menacing that Zoo flinched, his shoulders tensing as if a blade had sliced into them.

Caleb lowered his head so that Zoo could look into his eyes. "Zoo," he said, "my brother likes you. The next time you talk to your God, thank him for that."

Caleb released the hammer of his pistol, turned on his heel and walked out the door, stepping over the crumpled body of Zoo's armed guard on the way.

Over his shoulder, he said, "With me, Sam."

Samuel jumped and hurried after Caleb. In the doorway, he paused slightly, casting a worried glance back at Zoo, then he was gone.

In the aftermath of Caleb's departure, Zoo slumped all the way down to the floor, drained. His breath came in short, shivery gasps.

Kanna stood over him for a few moments, giving him some time to regain his senses. When Zoo's breathing had returned to a somewhat normal rhythm, Kanna grabbed him by the collar, pulled him up off the floor and dumped him into the captain's chair.

Zoo spent a few moments wiping his face with his sleeve. Finally, he seemed to realize that he was simply repeating the same circular motion over and over without effect. He took a deep breath and stopped. His eyes, fluttery and red, stared forward at nothing.

Satisfied that Zoo was tracking again, Kanna reached into a cigar box on the corner of the desk and selected a cigar. Zoo noticed. He fumbled in one of his drawers for a lighter and, even with shaky hands, managed to produce a flame. Kanna lit the cigar and took a deep draw, then blew perfect smoke rings at the ceiling.

"With Caleb, Zoo," he said, "you get one mistake. Just one. Hell and damnation are waiting for you if you make another." He winked down at the broken captain. "I like you, Zoo. I'm hoping you don't make another."

Kanna turned and walked to the door, cigar smoke billowing around him. At the door, he turned, catching sight of the baseball bat lying at Masu's feet. He reached down and picked it up, gently turning it so that he could read the etchings and the signature. He chuckled.

"By the way," he said with a smile, "this silly bat probably saved your life today. Whatever you paid for it, it was worth every bloody penny."

Kanna nodded to Masu, and the two men exited the room.

Alone in the room, Zoo stared at the door for a few long moments, as if he needed the time to make sure that Kanna and Masu were truly gone. Tears welled in his eyes. His breath caught in his throat, a soft stutter. With a sob, he dropped his head down to his desk and began to cry.

A few minutes later, on the Tavington ship, Caleb and Samuel stood together at the deck rail, watching the *St. Christopher* pull clear and start toward open sea. Samuel appeared small, as if the events of the day had diminished him somehow, whittled part of him away. He seemed unable to stand up straight.

Caleb glanced over, taking stock of his brother, noticing his ragged state. "Wishing you were back in Boston?" he asked, no trace of comfort in his voice.

Samuel stared down, unable to answer. Caleb gave the *St. Christopher* one last look, then turned from the rail and walked away. Samuel didn't even raise his eyes.

As the sound of Caleb's footsteps faded, Kanna walked up and put his arm around Samuel. "Don't worry your pretty little head about it, boyo," he encouraged, his voice light and casual. "Freetown in an hour. Make sure you look sharp. All of the fine folk'll be out in their Sunday go-to-meetin' clothes for Caleb." Samuel managed a nod.

Kanna held out the bloodstained baseball bat. "You forgot this," he said. Samuel clenched his jaw and took the bat from Kanna, who smiled and ruffled Samuel's hair. "A little soap and water and she'll be good as new," he promised. So saying, he gave

Samuel's shoulder a pat and started towards the stairwell. After a few steps, however, he turned his head back toward Samuel, watching the young Tavington for a few moments, genuine concern on his face.

For his part, Samuel didn't notice that Kanna had stopped. He simply stood, deflated, staring down at the bat in his hands. He turned it slowly, wiping at the blood, his eyes glossy and red.

Kanna sighed and walked away.

• • • •

The dying afternoon sun sparkled yellow and amber on the shifting ocean as the Tavington ship motored into a large bay, a natural coastal harbor. Surrounding the bay, a well-developed town spread outward from the water in orderly street grids, extending all the way into the low mountains beyond.

Caleb, Samuel, Masu and Kanna stood at the rail, Kanna ridiculous in a flashy multicolored silk suit and fedora, like a color-blind pimp who had just won the lottery. Caleb's appearance, by contrast, was severe and understated—a starched white dress shirt, black coat and trousers, black polished shoes. Masu mirrored Caleb's look, the only difference being the visible guns strapped to his left and right side. And the ever-present cigarette.

A long dock anchored the very center of the bay. It was solid and made to last, with space for a dozen ships to sit end to end, and wide enough to accommodate the machinery and vehicles necessary for loading and unloading. A secondary dock halfway to the shore split from the main one, offering an alternative landing point for vessels, as well as an overflow if needed.

This was obviously a town that depended on ships and the sea for its survival.

On the end of the main dock stood two men armed with automatic machine guns. They lifted their hands in greeting as the Tavington ship motored slowly by.

On the secondary dock, a line of men waited, eyes focused on the incoming ship. They were a hard-looking crew, but well dressed and impeccably groomed. Every single one was weighted down with weaponry, shoulder holsters, belt holsters—pistols and knives tucked and carried every which way. The dissonance was jarring—dark, obviously expensive suits combined with an arsenal for accessories, like bankers of the apocalypse.

Samuel took a deep breath. He remained somewhat subdued from the earlier encounter with Zoo Cali, but their approach to the town seemed to have lifted his spirits slightly. He scanned the dock and the shore, followed the buildings stretching into the gently rising mountains. A slow smile came to his face.

"Jesus, Caleb," he breathed. "I can't believe how much I've missed this place. I didn't think I would."

Kanna put his arm across Samuel's shoulder. "It's in your blood Sammy," he replied with a wide grin, "for better or worse."

Passo, once again at the wheel, slid the ship expertly into a soft landing directly in front of the waiting men.

As the ship's fenders touched home, a ramp was extended out from the dock.

Behind Caleb, the crew had assembled, forming two neat lines, each man standing straight and tall, dressed for the occasion. Caleb took a moment to survey his men, then focused his attention on the dock. He took one last look around him, stepped out and strode down the ramp like a king. Masu, Samuel and Kanna followed close behind.

The men on the dock moved forward as Caleb descended. One of them stepped clear of the others, obviously intending to be the first contact. He was a formidable-looking man, dressed well, in a dark suit and white shirt open at the collar, like Caleb. The skin under the shirt was black with tattoos. Both the man's ears sported gold hoops and diamond studs.

Caleb extended his hand, and the man took it.

"Luke," Caleb said in greeting.

"Caleb," came the response. "Good to see you, boy."

"And you. How is my father?"

Luke chuckled. "When he tells me, cousin," he said with a shrug, "I'll let you know. Good vacation?"

"Short."

Luke nodded. "I understand. Nice to have you back."

Caleb moved past Luke and down the dock. The group of men waiting held their positions, and Caleb simply gave them each a nod as he walked by.

Masu ignored everyone and shadowed Caleb.

As Caleb walked away, Luke turned to meet Samuel. "Sam. My God, boy, you've grown."

Samuel smiled and extended his hand. Luke, however, brushed it aside and grabbed the young Tavington up in a hard embrace. Samuel wheezed.

"It's good to see you, cousin Luke," he choked out. "It's good to be back."

"Christ," Luke responded, "are those muscles I feel under that coat?"

Luke set Samuel down. "Welcome back, boy," he said, slapping Samuel's shoulder.

Behind Samuel, the Tavington pirates had begun down the ramp. Kanna put his hand on Samuel's back and pushed him forward to avoid a traffic bottleneck.

Samuel made a movement as if to hurry after Caleb, but Kanna caught his arm. "Hang around, boyo," he said. "Your brother's off to see the wizard. You're with me, for now."

At the beach end of the pier sat several heavy-duty Land Rovers, windows tinted black. Around the Rovers, a group of men with short-barreled machine guns stood guard, eyes on Caleb and Masu as they approached.

Caleb climbed into the back seat of the first Rover. Masu slid into the front. Caleb sat for a few breaths, watching the activity continue out on the pier, his eyes focused mainly on Samuel.

Finally, he leaned forward. "Take me to Lord Nelson's," he said.

The driver of the Rover nodded, and the car pulled away from the water in a cloud of dust.

Caleb sat back, staring out the window at Freetown as the buildings passed by. He smiled.

Freetown was wild, a rough-riding, free-wheeling township of fearless men and women who lived dangerous lives. It was the wild west, a sprawling frontier village as colorful and hard-edged as Dodge City or Tombstone in their heyday.

The Rover made its way through the streets to the edge of town until it reached the beginnings of a low-rising section of foothills. The driver continued up the first section of sloping hillside, finally pulling to a stop in front of a large two-story structure situated with commanding views of the town and bay below. The front of the building looked exactly like an Old West Saloon, and a large sign above the double doors read "Lord Nelson's."

Masu jumped out of the Rover as soon as it stopped and opened Caleb's door. Caleb stepped out and followed Masu into the saloon.

Inside, Caleb took one step through the doors and stopped. Masu had already moved out of the entryway, his eyes scanning everything and everyone in the room.

Caleb surveyed the crowd in front of him through a thick haze of cigarette smoke. He gave a satisfied nod and breathed in deeply.

Lord Nelson's was the hardest saloon in the universe—Rikers Island with a two-drink minimum. The room was packed with people, a sea of wild tattoos, scar tissue, and enough guns to arm a small nation. It was a scene out of a madman's dream, a dystopian vision of life on the very edge of reality. There was nothing safe here, nothing stable, only a room full of potential—the potential for violence and danger. These were hard-edged characters from the underside of life, some good and some bad, roughnecks and stone-cold killers, all thrown together in the unmanaged and unmanageable wasteland called the Archipelago.

At Caleb's entrance, everyone's attention fixed immediately on him. A driving bass beat pounded out its rhythm as the room stood strangely still, their complete focus on the man standing at the door. Caleb held up his hand and the bartender killed the music.

"The Tavingtons," Caleb announced into the sudden silence, "would like to buy the house...until the sun."

The room erupted in a roaring cheer. Men and women crowded to the bar, all smiles and shouts in their good fortune. Caleb nodded to the bartender and the music started up again.

At the back end of the saloon, two armed guards stood at attention, one on either side of a massive metal door. The wall holding the door was built of solid wooden beams, unlike the rest of the saloon, which was wood paneling on top of hollow concrete blocks.

In spite of the fact that Lord Nelson's was packed with people, nobody came within five yards of the back wall, or the door it held.

Caleb and Masu made their way across the room and, even in their stampede to free liquor, the crowd was careful not to jostle Caleb, parting in front of him like the Red Sea. Respectful nods of greeting came from all in his path, and for one or two, Caleb slowed, allowing a more intimate connection and even a handshake.

As he and Masu neared the rear wall of the room, one of the armed guards knocked on the door, and it opened from the inside. Caleb walked through.

Once through the massive metal door, Caleb paused in the entryway and stared around the room. Behind him, Masu again stepped to the side.

The room that presented itself to Caleb couldn't have been more different than the one he had just left. It was as if he had been transported, away from the hard edge of the Archipelago and into the English countryside, to the stately manor of a noble house. It was a drawing room such as one could expect to find in the distinguished homes of the British aristocracy. In a word, the back room of Lord Nelson's Saloon was grand. High plastered ceilings sectioned and inlaid in the classical style, expensive artwork, gold-and-mahogany bar, antique mahogany tables and chairs, brocaded tapestries gilded in gold and the finest woven rugs over a floor of African darkwood.

The room was dim, lit only by candles, and very quiet. Two magnificent heavily tinted picture windows framed the ocean in the near distance. All in all, this was a room steeped in elegant, historical style, significant in its complete departure from the hard-scrabble world outside.

There was only one patron in the room, seated at a dining table near the windows. To attend this one patron, ten black-coated servants waited nearby. To guard him, six men stood at attention, one at every corner of the room and one beside each window, armed with short-barreled Uzi submachine guns and MK 23 Special Forces pistols. Sixteen men, plus the two guards on the other side of the door, all for one, lone diner—Alistair Tavington, Caleb's father and lord of the Tavington House.

Alistair Tavington was an average-sized man, with Caleb's strong features and the same intensity in his eyes. He had the bearing of an aristocrat, dignified and regal. There was nothing but substance in the man, nothing but solid significance.

Caleb made his way across the room to his father's table. His footsteps on the heavy African darkwood made barely a sound.

Alistair looked over from the window and watched his son's approach.

"Hello, Father," Caleb said.

Alistair smiled. He offered a hand from his seated position, and Caleb shook it. "Blessed be the sea that binds us, Caleb," he said, his voice low and steady.

"The sea that binds us, Father," Caleb responded. "You look well."

"And you. How was your trip?"

Caleb nodded. "It was fine, Da. Relaxing and quiet. Just the way I like it."

Alistair laughed. "Samuel?" he asked.

"He's very well. He'll be at the section later, getting reacquainted. I wanted to talk to you alone."

Alistair took a deep breath and leaned back slightly in his chair. "Ahhh, I see," he said. "You won't let him wander around, Caleb? He's been away from Freetown long enough…he might not remember where our section ends and Wallace's begins."

"I'll see to it," Caleb promised.

Alistair stared at his son's face for a moment or two, then extended his hand toward the chair opposite him. "You may sit, boy."

"Thank you, sir." Caleb pulled back the chair and sank down into it. Alistair continued staring into Caleb's face, then waved a waiter over.

"Bring the young master a Shano," he ordered. "Remind him what the Archipelago tastes like." He took a sip from his wineglass, then put it down with a soft chuckle. "So," he said, "this is it, then, Caleb? The big secret."

Caleb tilted his head back and gave his father a questioning look.

"Come on, boy," Alistair continued. "I've seen it for months: a big, burning…something. Just behind your eyes. The last time you looked like that, you left for almost two years—and came back with blood on your hands."

The waiter returned with an unlabeled bottle of cold, dark beer. Caleb took the bottle and drank a long swallow. He closed his eyes as he drank, savoring the taste of it.

Alistair nodded in approval. "Some things don't change, do they, Caleb?" he said. "Two hundred years of Tavington blood and sacrifice in that bottle…and every swallow still tastes like the near side of heaven. It's in your soul. Always will be."

He sighed.

"Now, what do you need to tell me?"

Caleb gathered himself. "I'm leaving, Father," he said. "I have to go."

"Again?"

Caleb shook his head. "For good. I can't stay here. I need to build a life...somewhere else."

Alistair considered this for a long moment, remarkably composed for a man whose world has just been turned on its head. Finally, he nodded and exhaled into a small laugh.

"I see," he said. "You know, Caleb, the fact that your mother couldn't stay in the Archipelago doesn't mean that no woman could."

"It's...complicated," Caleb answered with a sad smile.

"Yes, it always is."

Caleb took a deep breath. "It's Emma, Da," he said with a heavy voice. "It's Emma."

Alistair Tavington sat back, stunned, his composure finally cracked. His eyes were fixed and flat, shocked into stillness and disbelief.

"Jesus, God, Caleb," he breathed. "Jesus bloody God."

Caleb held his father's eyes in a steady gaze. "As I said...complicated."

Caleb's words drifted out into the silence. Both men simply sat then, frozen in the new world that had just been introduced. It was as if they were cast in stone, unmoving, as the day continued on without them for what seemed an age.

Finally, Alistair Tavington took a deep breath.

"Yes," he agreed. "I suppose you must go. There's...no other way." A smile came to his face, and there was genuine respect and admiration in it.

"You don't make easy choices, Caleb, but you certainly couldn't have made a better one. She's a fine young woman."

"Thank you, Father. I know she thinks the world of you."

"Have you told your mother?"

"Aye."

"And what did she say?"

Caleb paused for a moment before answering. "She said that you wouldn't keep me from the woman who could save my soul. She said you would remember that someone tried to save yours once."

Alistair nodded and laughed. "Well, you've been a grown man since you were twelve years old," he said, "so I'd be a fool to try to talk you out of anything now. Your mother always loved Emma, called her the jewel of the Archipelago, a rose among thorns."

Caleb leaned forward, his eyes searching his father's face. "Sam is here now, Father. He can stay."

"Don't trouble yourself about that, boy," Alistair said with a dismissive wave. "I managed to run this thing before you came along, and I might be able to stumble through after you're gone."

He shook his head, his eyes soft now.

"I'll miss you, Caleb. You'd be a stronger man than I if you stayed, but you'll be a better man than I if you go."

Alistair signaled to a waiter. "Bring us the best bottle of champagne we have," he said. "We've cause for a toast."

Caleb shook his head. "I'll think I'll finish the Shano, Father. It might be a long while before I have another. Perhaps you could join me."

Caleb reached for the bottle of beer on the table.

Alistair stared at the bottle, and the look on his face made it clear that he knew how important this moment was and that it should be recognized appropriately. He nodded.

"Perhaps I could. One last time for luck." He turned back to the waiter. "Shano it is."

CHAPTER SIX

On a gently sloping hillside facing the ocean, not far from the center of Freetown, stood the Cathedral of St. Brendan the Navigator. St. Brendan's presence was at once commanding and anomalous, its impressive architecture and grounds at strange odds with its prominent placement in a community of thieves and murderers. Given the quixotic balance of ideals versus reality, a church in a place like Freetown might be expected to sit empty. The pathways and pews of St. Brendan's, however, were strangely well worn. The residents of Freetown were regular attendees of mass and even visited St. Brendan's during the week for prayer. The priest, Father O'Hearne, was in great demand for home counseling and private meetings. Those living on the edge, it seemed, were eager to seek out the comfort that faith could provide.

The courtyard at St. Brendan's was well appointed and inviting, paved with cobblestones and large enough to host gatherings of hundreds. On this evening, it was packed with guests from the Tavington section of Freetown, a large crowd of men, women and children, all dressed in their finest. Tables overloaded with food filled the center of the space while chairs and benches had been set up throughout the church grounds. Lanterns hung on wires, crisscrossing above the cobblestones, giving the entire scene a festive air.

Armed men stood at every approach point, eyes alert.

As the day faded into evening, Caleb's Land Rover pulled up to the courtyard in a swirl of dust. The crowd reacted immediately, and a receiving line formed, starting near the edge of the courtyard and snaking back toward the church. After a few moments, Caleb exited the Rover and began to walk the line, shaking hands, sharing a word or two with each person. Masu faded into the crowd and eventually ended up on the church steps, keeping a careful watch on the proceedings.

A second Rover pulled up behind the first. Kanna, Luke and Samuel stepped out. Caleb paused and motioned for Samuel to join him, which created a stir among those gathered. The few who had already greeted Caleb rejoined the line so that they could shake Samuel's hand as well.

Kanna and Luke drifted along the edge of the crowd, finding a table set apart from the others. Luke nodded to a group of musicians, and they began to play. In a very short time, the party was in full swing—food, music and laughter the order of the evening.

Caleb retired to Luke and Kanna's table, leaving Samuel alone out in the crowd. Samuel was a natural at socializing, an easy smile always on his lips. A permanent knot of people surrounded him, laughing and talking, enjoying the young Tavington's company.

"He's just like Father," Caleb said to Kanna. "If you squint, you could imagine he is Father, the way the people respond to him."

"Aye," Kanna agreed. "They do love him...and they missed him. He has that same something that the old man has. People like to be near him."

Caleb nodded. "Tell him I'll see him later, Kanna. I'm going back. Keep him in our section of town, would you? I don't want him running into any of Black's gremlins tonight."

Caleb started to stand, but Kanna put his hand on Caleb's arm, stopping him in midmovement. "What's going on, Caleb?" he asked.

"What do you mean?" Caleb sat back down.

"I mean, your father moved heaven and earth to send Sammy off to that fancy American college...get him out of the killin' loop forever. You seem to be trying to get him back in."

"Life is unpredictable, Kanna," Caleb said. "Sam may be required to do what he has never been asked to do before."

Kanna shook his head and laughed. "Caleb," he said, "Sammy is good...and kind, but this life is not about goodness and kindness. It's about fear and death. I love you, Caleb boy, but when people look at you they see death and they remember fear. Anything less and Black bloody Wallace will own this ocean inside of a year."

Caleb leaned in close. He glanced around, as if to make sure that their voices couldn't carry to anyone nearby.

"Samuel chose on his own to come back here," he said in a hard whisper. "We all tried to talk him out of it. We didn't take on the security risk of sending a Tavington out into the world just to have him turn around and come straight back. We wanted him out." His voice dropped even lower. "I wanted him out."

Caleb paused. When he spoke again, there was a finality to his tone.

"But ultimately, Kanna, it's his choice. Not Father's and certainly not mine. If this is what he thinks he wants, then so be it. Sam's a Tavington. It's all he needs."

Kanna shrugged. "It's your world, Caleb...but Sam's not a Tavington like you're a Tavington."

Caleb stood again. "Things change, Kanna, that's all."

Then, in a voice that sounded as if he was trying to convince himself, he added, "Even in the Archipelago."

Caleb spun on his heel and followed Masu out of the church courtyard. Masu waved off the driver of the Rover and took his place in the driver's seat. Caleb climbed into the back.

They drove in silence toward the waterfront, their headlights illuminating an area of Freetown that was otherwise barely lit. Warehouses dominated the landscape here, lining both sides of the road and stretching to the water. Masu's eyes shifted carefully along their route, but there was no sign of activity in any direction. He angled the Rover through an alley alongside a series of dark loading docks, finally pulling up to a quiet stretch of buildings that seemed almost abandoned. A small broken-down dock stretched out into the water, shrouded in darkness except for a tiny light pole, its single bulb pushing a circle of yellow light into the vast black ocean all around. Everything else was just a shadow in the moonlight.

Caleb stepped out of the car and made his way onto the dock. He stood at the beach end of it, waiting, just outside the flickering circle of light. A flutter of movement from a nearby warehouse caught his eye. Out of the darkness walked Emma, and together, she and Caleb moved to the far end of the dock.

"Did you tell him?" Emma asked when they reached the water. Her voice was pensive and soft, swallowed by the unforgiving ocean in front of them.

Caleb nodded. "I told him."

Emma searched Caleb's face in the darkness. "And?"

"And he said I was a fool...if I stayed in the Archipelago when I could leave with you."

Emma's face stilled at the sound of Caleb's words. She stared up at him, the moonlight filling the distance between them like a whispery haze. Slowly, a smile came, and then she laughed with delight and threw her arms around Caleb. Her eyes filled with tears.

"Oh, Caleb," she said in a throaty whisper. "It's so wonderful." She took a deep, shaky breath, staring out at the dark water. "It didn't feel quite real, until just now," she said. "With his blessing, it seems almost possible, doesn't it?"

Caleb nodded. "With Father's blessing," he answered, "anything at all seems possible." He stepped back, held her at arm's length. "But I love you, Em, and that's always been real. Always."

Caleb's attention was drawn to the buildings fronting the water. He scanned the darkness, checked Masu's position.

Emma noticed his sudden change of focus. "My mother told me once," she whispered, "that the Archipelago is a jealous lover...that no man ever leaves."

Caleb's eyes remained fixed on the shadows. "Which is why we must go right away," he said. "Don't even pack. Leave everything."

Emma laughed, a sudden, giddy sound. "Are you sure, Caleb?" she asked.

"I'm sure," Caleb answered without hesitation. "If we delay, this place will test our resolve. I've seen it happen before. If we wait, the Archipelago will win...and we'll be waiting forever."

The tone in Caleb's voice gave Emma pause. "Everything here is always about forever," she said, her earlier giddiness evaporating in the face of Caleb's warning.

Caleb checked their surroundings again, found the glow of Masu's cigarette. "I'll send Masu tomorrow. Be ready Em."

Emma shook her head with a soft, sad laugh. "I've been ready to leave with you since I was fifteen, Caleb. One more night won't change a thing."

She pulled Caleb's face down into a kiss, and they stayed like that for a long moment, statues in a silent storm. When they finally stepped apart, she took a deep, steadying breath, then turned away and walked back down the dock. As Caleb watched, she turned into the shadow of a waterside warehouse and was swallowed by the darkness.

• • • •

The Tavington yacht sat dockside, only half-lit, two armed men standing guard by the gangplank. Caleb and Kanna stood at the bridge rail, unmoving, staring out at Freetown. Behind them in the shadows, the soft glow of a cigarette indicated Masu's presence as well.

The lights of an approaching Land Rover danced along the water. The car pulled up to the main dock and stopped. Samuel fairly jumped out, his demeanor much changed from the early hours of the day. There was a lightness to his step as he made his way to the ship, his jacket slung casually over his shoulder. He took the gangplank at a run and was standing at the bridge rail in no time at all.

"God," he gushed, "I've missed Freetown. How did I stay away for so long?" He clapped Kanna on the back and let out a loud whoop.

Caleb and Kanna both smiled at the younger Tavington's exuberance.

"I'd forgotten there were so many pretty girls here," Samuel continued. "I—"

A sharp three-toned whistle from the bow interrupted Sam's enthusiasm.

The smile died on Caleb's face. "Put your jacket on, Sam," he said, his tone somber.

Kanna cupped his hands to his mouth and yelled, "Lights."

The deck lights flashed on, bathing the scene in an eerie yellow-white, stark against the backdrop of the black ocean. Masu stepped further back into the shadow of the bridge.

Samuel slung his jacket around and slipped into it. As he stepped forward to the rail, Kanna turned him and straightened his collar, patting him on the cheek with a wink.

Motoring at an outbound angle to the main dock, a large yacht suddenly materialized out of the surrounding darkness, its dim running lights brightening as it passed. At the rail stood Black Wallace, his second-in-command, Tanner, his son, Michael, and his daughter, Emma. While the entire group stood at dignified attention, the look on Black's face was all contempt and simmering fury. Beside him, Emma seemed fragile and small, like a porcelain doll, at risk of falling and smashing into a thousand pieces. Her eyes riveted on Caleb's face. Even though the boats were separated by less than thirty yards, the distance between them seemed somehow endless, an unbridgeable chasm.

Caleb remained completely motionless, facing straight forward, but as the Wallace yacht slipped past the center of his line of vision, his eyes found Emma's for a brief moment. Even in the harsh light, and almost lost in the overbearing shadow of her father, she was dignified and beautiful. She gave Caleb a sad smile, and then the Wallace boat was away.

Caleb's shoulders slumped slightly, the barest acknowledgment of the weight they were carrying. He turned away from the rail.

"Get some rest, Sam," he said, his voice drained of life. "We'll be home soon."

CHAPTER SEVEN

In the conference room of the Wallace yacht, Black Wallace sat, heavy in his chair, whiskey tumbler close at hand, brooding over an open map book. A lit cigar added a layer of haze to the already dim, uninviting atmosphere. The room was claustrophobic, Black's dominating presence seeming to push everything else into a tighter, more restricted space.

A knock sounded and Black shifted his attention upward. Tanner stuck his head in.

"He's here," Tanner said.

Black nodded. "Get Michael first," he responded, "then bring him in."

Tanner closed the door. Black's gaze, however, didn't change. He remained fixed on the entryway. After a few moments, a shuffling heralded Michael's arrival.

"Come," Black said before there was even a knock.

The door opened and Michael stepped in. There was a look of apprehension on his face, the worried countenance of someone who felt perpetually hunted.

"You wanted to see me, Father?"

"Aye. Sit down and keep your mouth shut. We have a visitor."

Michael walked slowly forward and took a seat near his father at the table.

They sat in silence for a few moments, neither man looking at the other. It was as if they were strangers on a train.

The door opened and Tanner escorted in a man dressed in a rebel military uniform—Captain Wahroo—the same Indonesian rebel captain who had performed a dismissive pass-by of the Tavington yacht earlier in the day.

Tanner showed him to the table.

Two Wallace men entered immediately behind Wahroo and flanked the door. Tanner motioned to a chair opposite Black Wallace and indicated that Wahroo should sit. For his part, Wahroo hadn't taken his eyes off Black's face since entering the room. Even after Tanner's invitation, he paused, seeking some sort of confirmation from his host. Black nodded, and Wahroo sat down.

For the first time, Michael showed signs of life, his eyes widening in alarm as he noticed that Wahroo's spot at the table gave him a clear view of the open map book in front of Black Wallace.

Black leaned back in his chair, a look of clear, unadulterated disgust on his face. Wahroo squirmed under the malevolent glare.

Finally, Black broke the silence. "A man who is given power," he began, his voice a low growl, "often becomes very forgetful." Black let the words hang in the air for a few heavy moments. "What will you choose to forget, Captain, when the burden of power is thrust upon you?"

Wahroo seemed to gather himself. He sat as straight as he could in his chair. "I will forget nothing. I will honor all agreements."

Once spoken, the words died away into nothing, smothered by the overpowering weight of Black's presence.

Black leaned forward, a sneer on his face. "Of course you will," he said.

Unnerved, Wahroo didn't even try to meet the glare. He shifted his glance down and away. "And the dogs?" he asked.

Black smiled, amused. "Ah, yes. The legendary monsters of Sister Bay, trained to sniff out Indonesian rebels and swallow them whole." Black gave a derisive snort and glanced over at Tanner.

"We'll take care of them," Tanner said to Wahroo. "You just do your job, so my men can do theirs."

Black sighed, impatient. It was clear that Wahroo's presence was beginning to wear on him. He reached out, pushed the open map book toward Wahroo. Wahroo waited for a long second, then stood, leaned over the desk and closed the book.

Beside the desk, Michael's eyes widened in shock. He reached quickly into his belt, drew a short-blade knife and hurled himself at Wahroo, slashing in a wide, clumsy arc. The knife managed to gouge a deep line below Wahroo's right eye, and the two tumbled onto the floor. At impact, Michael lost his grip on the knife and it bounced across the hardwood. Wahroo scrambled away, but Michael caught him with a wicked right hook, then an elbow to the temple. Drops of Wahroo's blood sprayed onto the side of Black Wallace's desk.

Wahroo arched his back and threw Michael off him, then got to one knee and drew a gun from his waistband. Michael reached for the nearby knife.

Instantly, Tanner and the other two Wallace men had guns in their hands, pointing at Wahroo's head. Even in the frantic moment, Wahroo was alert enough not to raise his weapon. He froze in place, eyes locked on Michael.

Oblivious to anything else, Michael picked the knife up off the floor and lunged at Wahroo again. This time, Tanner stepped in and casually pushed the young Wallace aside.

Behind the desk, Black Wallace yawned. "Stop," he said. "Take your seat, Michael," Black continued.

Michael shook his head. "Father," he panted, "the book. He has to die."

"Take your seat, boy. Don't make me tell you again."

Black Wallace directed his gaze toward Wahroo. The captain's hand still held his pistol, and it was now shaking with rage. The rest of him, however, remained frozen in place under the guns of the Wallace men. The cut on his cheek was gushing blood, and his face was beginning to swell as a result of Michael's blows.

Black gave Wahroo a tight smile. "Put your gun away, Captain," he said.

Wahroo swallowed hard. "What...is...going on?" he asked, his voice strained.

"I'm sorry," Black answered, and there wasn't even a tiny bit of sincerity in the apology. "It seems that I forgot to mention our little arrangement to my son."

Black nodded to Tanner. All three of Black's men lowered their guns.

"Arrangement?" Michael sputtered. "What arrangement? What...are you talking about, Father?"

Black ignored Michael. "I hope he didn't hurt you too badly," he said to Wahroo. "Fortunately, he's never been worth a shit with a knife."

Tanner laughed, a short, greasy bark that gave an eerie echo in the room.

For his part, Wahroo wasn't seeing the humor in the situation. His face, now puffy on one side, was set in a mask of anger. He got up, moving slowly so as not to set anyone off, and took a short step to the side of the table. Eyes on Michael, he reached down and picked up the map book.

"Get your hands off that," Michael screamed. "Goddamn it."

Michael struggled to his feet, knife still in hand.

Wahroo clutched the map book to his chest and took a step backwards, away from Michael.

"Michael," Black Wallace said. "Sit down and shut up."

"Father—"

"Shut up, boy."

Tanner slid forward a step, blocking Michael's path to Wahroo.

Michael looked frantically around the room, his gaze flitting from Wallace man to Wallace man, all of whom seemed content to let Wahroo hold the book.

"No," Michael moaned. "Father, what are you doing?"

Black Wallace ignored his son. He gave a nod to Wahroo. Upon seeing this, Wahroo placed the map book under his arm and turned toward the door.

"Noooo," Michael screamed and rushed at Wahroo again. Tanner jumped into his path, spun him around and put him in a headlock.

"No." Michael's voice broke as his windpipe closed down. "Tanner, no. What the hell is going on? Father, no."

He thrashed wildly in Tanner's headlock and managed to focus his attention on the other two Wallace men.

"Stop him," he choked out. "Stop him. Are you insane?"

Behind his desk, Black Wallace watched Michael with a look of absolute contempt on his face. He nodded again to Wahroo, who had paused in his exit. With this final confirmation from Black, however, Wahroo continued on, took one last look at Michael, and then disappeared through the door.

"No," Michael sobbed, tears running down his face, now. His body went limp.

Still keeping the headlock, Tanner dragged Michael to his original chair, then dumped him into it. As soon as Michael hit the chair, however, he bounced back up, knife in hand, and attacked Tanner.

Without any concern, Tanner fended off the knife thrust, disarmed Michael and kicked him back into his chair.

"What have you done?" Michael asked, his voice wavering. "Why?"

Black Wallace exhaled loudly. "Do you really want to know why, boy?" he asked. "Because Caleb Tavington is ten times the man you are. That's why. Because if something happens to me, he will own this ocean in six months. That's why. Because he befouled my family. That's why."

Black's speech was low and menacing, and his eyes were focused hard on his son.

Michael returned his father's glare with hatred. His jaw worked soundlessly as his mind struggled with what he had seen. He turned to Tanner.

"You just committed suicide, Tan," he said. "The Council will hang you. They'll hang both of you." He directed his attention to the men at the door. "They'll hang all of you. What have you done? You've destroyed us."

Tanner shook his head and sat down in a seat across from Michael.

"One man who knows the book can't destroy us, boy," he said. "We're one well-placed bullet from being right where we were before."

"What are you talking about?" Michael's voice rose in exasperation. "He'll tell all of them. He'll show all of them. They'll know all of the reefs. No one will be safe."

"He'll tell no one," Black Wallace interjected.

"What?"

"If someone gave you a gift that made you God, would you share it?"

Michael stared at his father for a long moment, confused.

"That book," Black continued, "makes him God. He'll memorize every page and then destroy it."

Michael exhaled slowly, the adrenaline draining out of him, leaving only weariness behind. "The Council...," he started, but he didn't seem to have the energy to finish.

Black Wallace snorted. "I am the Council, boy," he said with venom. "The Wallace family built the Council, do you understand? But the Tavingtons go about their business as if they own us, as if the Council is their lapdog...and when Alistair Tavington is gone, the devil that is his son will use the Council to put us at the bottom of the ocean"—a sheen of glossy hate glimmered in Black's eyes as he spoke—"and I will not allow it."

Michael shook his head, exhausted, broken. "Father, what you've done is wrong. It goes against everything..."

He stood suddenly, taking his father and Tanner by surprise. Both men flinched involuntarily at the unexpected movement.

Michael looked at Tanner and continued speaking, his voice heavy. "We've lived our whole lives under the code, Tan...protect the book with your blood. You swore it on your honor...and you just sat there and watched that filthy mutt put his hands on it."

Tanner clenched his jaw for a moment, and it was clear in his eyes that he knew Michael was right. "If it makes you feel any better," he said, "when this is all over, I'll cut his hands off for you myself."

Michael closed his eyes and began reciting from memory. "Knowledge of the reef is a sacred trust."

Tanner cut Michael off. "I know the law, boy," he said brusquely.

"It's more than a law, Tanner," Michael rejoined. "A code of honor is all that separates us from monkeys like Wahroo."

Black snorted, watching Michael with an expression of disgust on his face.

Tanner held his hand out to Michael, a gesture of conciliation. "Sleep it off," he said, and his tone was not unkind. "It'll make sense in the morning."

"Never," Michael responded. "It'll never make sense...and you know that as well as I do. You've broken the code...you've ruined us...you're—"

"Enough," Black Wallace growled, out of patience.

Michael stopped talking immediately. He looked from Tanner to his father, his eyes pleading, imploring, searching. Finding nothing of comfort in either man, he dropped his head and shuffled out of the room.

As the door closed behind Michael, Tanner lit a cigarette. He watched the smoke drift up and away, his expression somber. "We're committed now," he said. "The unforgivable sin." He laughed, a grim sound that had nothing of mirth in it. "It's a shitty thing," he continued. "Pissin' away honor...for a shot at the title."

Black Wallace watched his second-in-command closely. "Don't dwell on it, Tanner. The sun will still rise tomorrow."

Tanner looked over and stared, unflinching, into Black's eyes. He pushed himself slowly to his feet. "Don't worry about me," he said. "I'm in till the dying's over. I hate them that much." He walked to the door, smoke trailing behind him like a boat's wake. "But it is a shitty thing," he finished.

Pausing in the entryway, he stubbed out his cigarette on the doorjamb, then left the room.

• • • •

The Tavington yacht cut through the black sea, shimmering in the moonlight like a ghost in the mist. Behind it lay the vast dark expanse of the Archipelago. Ahead, a coral island, high cliffs rising on all sides save the very center, which offered a large inlet bay. Lights glinted along the shore.

Caleb and Samuel stood at the bridge rail, casual in long-sleeve silk shirts open at the collar. Their attention was focused on the island. Just outside of the entrance to the bay, a glint of moonlight on metal betrayed the presence of a small ship.

Samuel squinted. "They're waiting for us," he said.

As Samuel said the words, the Tavington yacht began to slow its approach.

Caleb nodded. His eyes scanned the ship at the bay's entrance.

"Is Tasi there?" Samuel asked.

"Tasi is always there," Caleb said, then lifted his hand and pointed to a spot ahead. "Now, pay attention, Sam. Do you remember the cut?"

Samuel checked the lights on shore for his bearings.

Caleb shifted his hand. "The small tower...the large tower. Don't let the lights fool you. Ignore the large tower and the entrance is just off the small one. Right...now."

The yacht veered sharply, knocking Samuel off-balance. He reached out and grabbed the deck rail, steadying himself as the engines reduced speed even more and the yacht motored into the bay. He looked down, along the side of the ship. Less than three feet below the surface, so close to the hull that a man could reach out and touch it, he could see reef, visible in the deck lights.

"And at this marker," Caleb continued, pointing to another spot on the shore, "we turn again, this time at a forty-five-degree angle."

"Okay...I remember," Samuel said. "But, getting here, I don't remember any of the reefs."

"Not many do. That's why they're in the book. You'll get comfortable with it, eventually."

Samuel watched the razor-sharp reef stream by, just below the water's surface. "Why don't we just use sonar, Caleb?" he asked.

Behind them, Kanna snorted in disgust. He rolled his eyes with dramatic flair. "Because we're sailors, boyo," he said, "not bloody bass fishermen, for God's sake. Depth finders are useless on the reef at speed."

Caleb nodded. "And on this water, Sam...in the Archipelago, if they're useless at speed, they're useless to us."

Kanna stepped to the rail and put his arm on Samuel's shoulder. "None of that electronic piddle's worth a shite out here, Sammy. A man who's good on the water'll sail a hole through your ass while you're still fumblin' for the on/off switch."

Samuel laughed, his eyes now sweeping the bay ahead.

Caleb turned to face him. "Welcome home, Sam," he said, his voice serious and low.

The Tavington yacht entered the bay. As it cleared the reef, the onshore lights brightened, giving clear outline to six other large yachts already harbored in the bay. All six were identical to Caleb's yacht.

Caleb's yacht motored in slowly, easing through the still water to a docking point at the far end of the line of waiting yachts. As the Tavington men secured the yacht to the dock, the small ship that had been waiting outside the reef made its way through the cut and directly to the side of the Tavington yacht.

Caleb turned from the rail and took the stairs down to the main level.

On the deck of the small ship stood a Malaysian man, Tasi, who looked so much like Masu that the two were obviously brothers. Tasi was dressed only in a simple sarong, a long-handled blade sheathed at his side. Around his neck hung a small gray stone on a leather necklace.

Except for his face, every inch of his skin was covered with wild, colorful tattoos, distinctly Malaysian in their patterns, thickly layered and striking, even in the shadowy moonlight.

Caleb walked out onto his deck. All eyes, Tavington and otherwise, were on him. He raised his right hand in greeting.

Within seconds, Tasi and a dozen of his men had climbed onto the Tavington yacht and stood in a line facing Caleb. Among those watching, not a sound could be heard.

Tasi walked forward and stopped when he was standing directly in front of Caleb. "God, in his wisdom, has allowed the mother to bring us together again." Tasi's voice was steady and low, his English perfect, with just the faintest trace of an accent.

Caleb smiled. "She gives and she takes," he said. "Blessed be the sea that binds us."

All of the Malaysian warriors were standing perfectly still, frozen in respectful silence.

On the bridge, Samuel and Kanna watched the scene down on the deck.

Samuel glanced at the shoreline, where a crowd was gathering, women and children, all watching Caleb and the Malaysians.

"How did Tasi know when Caleb would be back?" Samuel asked.

"Hell if I know, boy," Kanna responded. "The two are linked in a strange way."

On deck, Caleb and Tasi embraced each other. As they stepped apart, Tasi drew his blade. One of the men behind him produced a carved wooden bowl fastened to ropes. He lowered the bowl down into the water, let it fill, and retrieved it.

Caleb pulled his shirt over his head, revealing in the deck lights his entire upper body, covered with tattoos identical to Tasi's.

Around his neck, Caleb wore a necklace of gray stone on a leather thong.

The man with the bowl of seawater walked forward and set it down in between Tasi and Caleb. Tasi handed Caleb the blade.

"What's going on?" Samuel asked.

"It's a Keyowah custom, Sammy boy. Caleb's their version of Jesus...this is like church for them."

Caleb used Tasi's knife to open a thin cut on the underside of his forearm. He held the cut above the bowl, and blood began to drip down into the seawater. He handed the blade back to Tasi, who performed the same action, adding his blood to the water in the bowl. After Tasi, the blade was passed to a nearby Masu, who also cut his forearm and dripped his blood into the bowl. Then, one by one, each Keyowah man did the same.

"What was it about, Kanna?" Samuel wondered out loud. "The Pawan war. Nobody will tell me anything about those days...and I was too young to remember. Why did Caleb go?"

"I don't know why Caleb went," Kanna said. "Nobody knows. He just went. He just...he's just...Caleb."

"But why him? An Englishman, leading the Keyowah? And he was only fifteen years old when he left."

Kanna shrugged. "Tasi told me once that they believe Caleb is the reincarnation of their greatest chief...that he was sent to them by the mother...the ocean...to fight the Pawan. As far as they're concerned, there's God, then there's Caleb."

On the deck below, the bloodletting ceremony was finished.

In solemn silence, the Keyowah warriors formed a ring around the bowl of salt water and blood. Each man sat down cross-legged on the deck and took off his necklace—all leather thongs holding gray stones. With care, they placed them into the bowl.

Tasi began to chant in Malay, low and cadenced, and each man's head nodded gently to the rhythm of it. Then, with Tasi's soft chant filling the space within the circle, Caleb reached into the bowl and pulled out a necklace. One by one, every man did the same, in clockwise order around the circle. Finally, it was Tasi's turn, and the chant ended when he had reached in and retrieved the last necklace. He let his gaze sweep all of the men in the circle, then uttered a single word. At this word, they all slipped the necklaces over their heads and dropped them down into place around their necks.

"They take the first necklace they touch," Kanna explained, "and carry each man's blood next to their heart. It reminds them that they are all responsible for each other...that they are all brothers."

The Keyowah slowly got to their feet. Then, in silent clockwise order, each man held his rifle out to Caleb.

"They want Caleb to bless their rifles," Kanna said, glancing over at Samuel to make sure he was tracking along. "It's the most important thing that a Keyowah warrior owns. They are never separated from it...they sleep with it, bathe with it...die with it. And no one can shoot like a Keyowah warrior. No one."

Caleb placed his hand on each Keyowah rifle and spoke words in Malay.

"Is it true what they say, Kanna?" Samuel asked. "All of the...terrible things? Did Caleb really—"

"Sammy, it was a war," Kanna interrupted. "Bad things happen in wars."

On deck, the Keyowah ceremony had come to an end.

Caleb looked up at the bridge, then over toward the nearby shore. He raised his arm above his head and swirled it around.

It was as if he had announced the start of a race. Out of the shadows, Tavington men flooded the deck, whooping and yelling into the night. Several simply ran right off the end of the ship and into the water. On the shore, the waiting crowd surged into the ocean to meet the returning Tavington sailors: their husbands, fathers, brothers and sons.

Bonfires all along the shore burst suddenly into flame, reflecting off the black water into the even blacker sky. Caleb nodded to Passo, who was standing next to a contained bonfire cylinder. Passo smiled, lit a match and dropped it into the container. Within seconds, the deck was awash with flickering yellow light from Passo's fire.

Music began to play, from a dozen different places. Laughter and song echoed into the night.

Caleb stared through the flames of Passo's fire, scanning the neighboring yachts, coming to rest on one in particular. On the bridge of that yacht, Alistair Tavington stood, partially hidden in the shadows, glass in hand.

Caleb smiled and nodded an invitation to his father. Alistair returned the smile but shook his head. Instead, he raised his glass to his son.

Caleb turned to his own bridge and waved Samuel down.

"A summons from His Majesty," Kanna said. Samuel laughed and rushed out, hitting the stairs at a run. "Don't touch their rifles, boyo," Kanna shouted after him. "They get all flustered if you do."

Kanna scanned the deck below, then the surrounding yachts, and finally, the shoreline. He breathed in deeply, as if savoring the moment. All around, the welcome party was in full, raucous swing. Kanna smiled, turned away from the window and started down the stairs.

CHAPTER EIGHT

The dawn broke clear and sudden across the Archipelago, rushing in without preamble to light the horizon, as if a great hand had simply brushed away the darkness. The black expanse of ocean turned a shimmering blue in scant minutes, and the cold night air fled without a fight before the warming sun.

In the bay sheltering the Tavington yachts, the aftermath of the night's party was evident: groups of men and women sleeping on the beach, and scattered across Caleb's deck. The once-raging bonfires continued to push tendrils of wispy smoke into the new morning. Empty bottles littered the landscape. From all outward appearance, this had been a celebration of epic proportion.

The Keyowah warriors were asleep on the deck of their own yacht, each one with a firm grip on his rifle.

All was quiet, save the gentle lapping of waves upon the sand.

Below deck on the Tavington yacht, Caleb lay on his bed, wide awake, staring at the ceiling. His eyes were red-rimmed and bloodshot, and it was obvious that he hadn't slept at all during the night.

With a sigh, he sat up. On the opposite wall, a mirror gave him the opportunity to stare at himself. After a long moment, he grimaced and rubbed at the tattoos on his arms, as if they could come off.

The morning sun filtered into his cabin. He watched dust particles drift in the light, then walked to the porthole window and flung it open, staring out into the new day.

• • • •

On the shoreline at the far end of the bay, a Tavington guard slept soundly, empty bottle nearby. Several yards away, a ground-mounted M82 antimateriel rifle faced the entrance to the bay, protecting the yachts within. Lying across the guard's chest, his MP5 submachine gun rose and fell gently with every breath.

Not far in front of the sleeping guard sat Tanner, Black Wallace's second-in-command. At Tanner's side knelt a massive vicious-looking dog, a mix of Newfoundland and mastiff, easily tipping the scales at three hundred pounds and half Tanner's height at its shoulder. Beside the gigantic animal, Tanner seemed as small as a child. At the moment, the dog was half-dozing as Tanner scratched it under the chin.

"Good boy," Tanner murmured. He reached into his pocket and produced a chunk of dried meat. The dog took it eagerly, its huge jaws making short work of the morsel.

In Tanner's other hand, he held an MK 23 with a silencer attached.

Tanner focused on the sleeping guard. "Slade," he said.

Slade stirred.

"Slade, wake up."

Slade's eyes opened. He blinked several times, then tried to sit up, confused.

"Tanner?" he said, his voice thick.

Tanner smiled and continued scratching under the dog's chin. "Mornin', Slade."

Slade finally sat all the way up. He looked around, trying to get his bearings. "What the hell are you doing here?" he asked.

Tanner lifted his MK 23. "Killing you."

Casually, without making a sudden motion and while still scratching the dog, Tanner fired his weapon. Slade jerked and crumpled back down onto the ground.

Tanner put his head down next to the dog's head. "Good boy. I'm sorry."

Tanner pressed the gun gently into the dog's chest and pulled the trigger. The dog gave a soft yelp, then slumped to the ground. Tanner held its head and gently laid it down.

"I'm sorry," he repeated.

· · · ·

Moments later, Tanner was crouched at the base of a sandy slope, assembling a high-powered sniper rifle. Movement from nearby drew his attention, and he spotted another Wallace man, John Horn, running in a low crouch toward him. Horn carried a long-range rifle of his own.

He came to a sliding halt beside Tanner.

"Who was it?" Horn asked.

"Slade."

Horn snorted. "I don't give a shit who the man was, Tan," he growled. "Tell me which dog."

Tanner clenched his jaw. "Shakespeare," he said through his teeth.

"Goddamnit," Horn breathed. "Shake was my favorite."

"Who was it for you?"

"Pixie."

"And the man?"

"Bayer. Sound asleep." Horn smiled and dug an elbow into Tanner's side. "Just like old times, huh?"

Tanner laughed and stood.

The two men ran up the slope behind them in a crouch, rifles at the ready. They crested the hill, revealing a wide-open view of the Tavington yachts in the bay below.

Both men immediately directed their attention to the open ocean beyond the bay.

Outside of the Tavington reef sat six large yachts, all flying rebel colors. A seventh yacht waited several hundred yards further out.

"What the hell are they waitin' for?" Horn asked, breath coming in short gasps from his sprint up the hill. "They should have been in the gap by now."

Tanner shook his head, frustration and anger written clearly on his face. "Damn it. That monkey waited too long." He glanced nervously at the Tavington ships in the bay, then checked the sun's position on the horizon. "Go," he ordered.

Horn scrambled away in a crouching run along the ridge that brought him to a point directly above Alistair Tavington's yacht. He took a few moments to mount his sniper rifle in place, then gave Tanner a thumbs-up.

Tanner nodded, set up his own rifle and settled down into position. Once again, he checked the rebel boats, and the sun.

"Goddamnit," he said, with only the wind and sand to hear him. With a long exhale, he focused on Caleb's yacht and sighted down the scope.

· · · ·

On the rebel yacht furthest from the Tavington bay, Captain Wahroo stared out of his bridge window, face still puffy from Michael Wallace's punches. A large bandage covered most of his left cheek, extending to a line of broken skin just under his eye.

Standing nearby, one of Wahroo's lieutenants focused intently on the six rebel yachts just outside of the reef.

Wahroo put a high-powered monocular to his eye. He scanned the bay, stopping briefly at the two towers and the shore markers. With one final sweep of the Tavington yachts, he picked up a radio.

"Begin," he said into the static and silence. "God is with you. Begin." Wahroo bowed his head. His lips moved in a silent prayer.

Outside the reef, the first of the rebel ships began to motor toward the gap. Slowly, then with increasing speed, it sliced through the water, its powerful engines coming to life with a growling hum. One by one, the other rebel ships followed suit, maneuvering into line directly behind the first and ramping up to speed.

Wahroo finished his prayer and lifted his head. "Sleep soundly, demon-child," he said, his voice soft but charged with anticipation. "Sleep forever." Eyes focused firmly on the ships approaching the gap, he handed the radio over to his lieutenant. "Freetown," he said.

The lieutenant received the radio with a nod. He held it up to his mouth and spoke into it. "Section two," he said, "we are underway. You may begin your assault."

Wahroo muttered under his breath, continuing his prayer.

"Show no mercy," the lieutenant added. "They would have none for you."

• • • •

Caleb stared out of his bedroom window, eyes unfocused. From his vantage position, he could see a small early section of the gap in the reef. Still, as the lead rebel boat slipped through the small opening, Caleb almost missed it. At the last, it was a wink of reflected sunlight that caught his eye, and he turned.

"Mother of mercy," he whispered in shocked disbelief.

Spinning on his heel, he was at the door in a split second, then through it and into the hallway. Scrambling to the stairwell, he leaped over a sleeping sailor and slammed a red disk high on the hallway wall. A siren blared, and red lights began flashing through the ship.

All around, sleeping men reacted to the alarm. Bleary-eyed and disoriented, they nonetheless jumped to action. For men like these, responding well to emergency moments often meant the difference between life and death. When it was required, they could fill the breach, even with their heads full of fog and eyes full of grit.

"To arms," Caleb shouted at the top of his lungs. "We're under attack."

Caleb dashed up the stairs and sprinted for the bridge, jumping over men and women, or simply shouldering them out of his way.

Once in the bridge, he scanned the gap in the reef. The lead rebel ship was almost halfway through. The others were not far behind.

"Christ," he breathed.

Passo stumbled into the bridge, eyes wide.

"Clear the boat, Passo, now," Caleb ordered. "Everybody into the water." Caleb fired up the engine.

Passo spun around and disappeared back through the entryway, screaming orders. As the door closed, Masu slipped through and stood, quietly at the ready.

Caleb hit the button on the ship's PA system. "All hands, abandon ship," he announced. "Abandon ship."

He checked the position of the rebel boats in the gap, then braced himself as he slammed the yacht into gear. The ship lurched forward and away from the dock, tearing out the stay lines. The men and women on board staggered at the sudden movement, their equilibrium lost, adding to the chaos around them. Disoriented and off-balance, they stumbled to the deck rails, diving or falling into the water.

On the deck, a shirtless, profanity-spewing Kanna screamed out orders, pushing anyone he could get his hands on, shepherding the crew off the ship.

• • • •

On the ridge above the Tavington bay, Tanner slid his crosshairs back and forth, sweeping Caleb's deck and bridge, waiting for his shot.

"Come on, boy," he whispered. "Come on." He allowed himself to glance quickly at the rebel ships. "Shit. Come on, boy."

His hands on the rifle began to sweat under the pressure of holding the weapon steady in the growing Archipelago heat. His grip tightened. Along his forehead, small beads of sweat began to form. He blinked his eyes and took a slow, deep breath.

Meanwhile, on the open ocean, Captain Wahroo flinched when he heard the alarm sound on Caleb's yacht. He checked the rebel boats, all still in the gap. He put the radio to his mouth.

"Open fire," he ordered, his voice strangely tight. "All guns. Kill everything."

On board the rebel yachts, the .50-caliber deck guns opened fire, unleashing a hail of bullets at the Tavington boats. The guns rained chaos down on their targets, splintering boats, chopping up the water, cutting men to pieces. It was like shooting paper targets in an arcade. With no cover and no long-range weapons at their disposal, the Tavington men and women were wide open and at the rebels' mercy.

On the Malay boat, however, the tattooed warriors reacted quickly—no panic, no hurry, rifles at the ready. They snapped awake, immediately alert. With no wasted movement, they jumped into the shallow water, holding their weapons above their heads, and waded to shore. Tasi flashed hand signals and the men sprinted up a small slope, toward defensible firing positions.

Alistair Tavington rushed onto the deck of his yacht, automatic rifle in hand, his eyes still bleary from sleep.

On the ridge above the bay, John Horn smiled, centering his crosshairs on Alistair Tavington's chest. "Good night," he whispered and gently squeezed the trigger.

The suppressed muzzle made barely a sound as the round left it.

The impact of the bullet stopped Tavington in midstride, crumpled him into himself and threw him back like a discarded rag doll. He landed in a twisted heap near the deck rail, his rifle spinning away, overboard and into the ocean.

From their new positions, Tasi's Keyowah warriors spotted the discharge of smoke from John Horn's rifle. Without even a split second of hesitation, the group reacted as one, spinning their rifles around and opening fire on Horn's position. One of the warriors spotted Tanner on the far side of the ridge and targeted him as well.

The instant Keyowah response took Horn completely by surprise. Before he had even begun to withdraw from his position, he was hit several times and thrown backwards down the ridge.

On the far side, a Keyowah bullet caught Tanner in the shoulder. Spun around by the impact, he rolled down the back side of the ridge, finally sliding to a stop near the base. Shaking his head to gather himself, he staggered to his feet and ran hard away from the gunfire.

Two of the Keyowah warriors peeled off from the group and sprinted up the slope toward the rim of the ridge.

Tasi watched them go, then turned his attention back to the bay.

The first rebel ship had already cleared the reef, its guns obliterating Caleb's men in the water, tearing up the Tavington boats.

Moving in a direct intercept line to the gap, Caleb's yacht powered toward the invading rebel ships, its engines roaring. The decks were now mostly clear of passengers.

The door flew open with a crash and Passo burst in, eyes wild, a pistol in either hand. Masu stepped away from the entryway.

Caleb turned. "You too, Passo," he said, his voice strangely calm amidst the insanity and noise. "Get off."

Passo shook his head, sweat spraying from his face. "We're sitting ducks in the water, Caleb."

Caleb grimaced. "Those ships clear the reef, we're sitting ducks wherever we are. Now, get off."

Passo nodded and rushed out.

Out in blue water, Wahroo focused through his monocular. He watched Caleb's yacht moving toward the gap in the reef. His eyes widened in alarm. He snatched up the radio. "Blow that boat out of the water," he screamed into the receiver. "Stop that boat."

Back on the Tavington yacht, Caleb scanned the deck below him. Only Kanna and Samuel remained. Kanna stood tall at the rail, emptying a pair of pistols at the rebel boat that had cleared the reef. When each gun clicked empty, he hurled them at the offending target, then looked up at the bridge.

Caleb motioned with his hand. Kanna nodded. He grabbed Samuel by the shirt and the two leaped off the side of the ship into the water.

The rebel boats began to concentrate their fire on Caleb's yacht in an attempt to cripple it in the water and prevent it from reaching them. Caleb and Masu crouched behind the map table as the bridge disintegrated around them. Still, the yacht hurtled toward the gap in the reef.

As the powerful .50-cal rounds obliterated glass and wood and metal, Caleb met Masu's eyes. "I need a touch mine, brother," he said.

Masu exhaled a thin stream of smoke and nodded. Caleb dove through the entryway and down the stairs to the deck. Masu flicked his cigarette toward the shattered remains of the windows, then followed Caleb down the stairs.

Up on the ridge, the Malay sharpshooters were unleashing a steady stream of deadly fire from their elevated positions, emptying clips rapidly, hammering at the soldiers manning the rebel .50s.

On his yacht, Wahroo could see the effect that the Keyowah warriors were having on his ships. He scanned the decks in horror. With the accurate deadly fire coming from Tasi's men on the ridge, only half of his .50-caliber guns were still firing at Caleb.

"Destroy that boat," he screamed into the radio. "Destroy that boat." The Tavington yacht continued its intercept line. Wahroo exhaled in a long, shuddering sigh. "God save us," he breathed.

On the Tavington yacht, Caleb had reached the engine room. In his hand, he held a safety flare. He took one last look at the reef. The second rebel boat was only meters from clearing the gap and entering the bay.

"Masu," he shouted, then sparked the flare and threw it down into the engine room.

Below deck, near the bow end of the hull, Masu was hurriedly attaching a limpet touch mine to the inner armor plating of the ship. He snapped the magnetic backing of the limpet onto the steel barrier, the touch-sensitive disc on its surface pointed toward the very tip of the bow—the impact point. He twisted the limpet, arming it, and ran for the ladder to the deck.

Above deck, Caleb eyed the distance to the second rebel boat and gave a grim smile. Shielding his eyes from the splintering wood and exploding glass fragments all around him, he sprinted toward the stern of the ship. From the stairwell, Masu appeared and shadowed Caleb at a dead run.

As the Tavington yacht hit the gap in the reef at full speed, Caleb and Masu launched themselves over the stern rail and into the ocean below.

With a booming crash, the Tavington yacht plowed into the second rebel boat before it cleared the reef. The scream of twisting, crumpling steel and fiber-reinforced plastic echoed across the water.

As the metal folded into itself, the limpet mine at the bow of the Tavington boat detonated, setting off a reaction with the engine room flare. Both boats exploded into flames, sealing the gap in the reef.

Caleb and Masu hit the water cleanly and surfaced. Pieces of burning debris rained down all around them. A large black plume of smoke billowed from the wreckage of the two ships.

The remaining rebel boats in the reef were trapped, the gap being too small for anything but a one-way trip straight through.

In the bay, multiple Zodiacs had been launched from shore, and a rescue operation was underway even as the gunfire continued. The injured Tavington men and women were being pulled from the water, along with the dead. Those who remained among the living had climbed aboard the large Tavington yachts, which were now motoring slowly toward the rebel ships trapped in the gap. Soaked Tavington men assembled on the decks of these yachts, armed with high-powered automatic weapons from each ship's armory.

Kanna stood on the deck of the closest yacht to the reef, dripping wet, bleeding from a head wound. Behind him, men began to strap into the turrets of the .50s. All around, heavily armed men rushed to the rails.

Kanna held up a fist. The men waited. On every Tavington yacht, they kept their eyes on Kanna's upheld fist.

The ships came to a slow stop, idling in a line facing the gap in the reef.

The Malay sharpshooters continued their strafing of the lone rebel ship that had cleared the reef into the bay. Weak return fire came from one or two of the ship's doorways and portholes. The on-deck .50-caliber guns had long since been abandoned.

Kanna waited until Caleb was well clear of the gap and out of the line of fire, then dropped his fist in an emphatic chop.

Every .50-cal Tavington gun opened fire, along with dozens of handheld machine guns. On both sides of Kanna, men stepped to the rail with rocket launchers and fired.

The rebels in the gap were obliterated. The concentrated Tavington firepower demolished the trapped ships, reducing them to splintered, listing wrecks as the men on board abandoned ship.

Far out to sea, on the remaining rebel yacht, a stunned Wahroo lowered his monocular. The lieutenant at his side reached over, grabbed the monocular and surveyed the scene. He breathed out a long, trembling breath.

"Tavington lives," he whispered, the weight of the words seeming to push all of the air out of his lungs.

Wahroo stepped away from the window and sat down at the map table. His shoulders slumped and he stared blankly at the far wall.

The lieutenant swept the bay from side to side, then rested his vision on the Malay sharpshooters, who still had command of the ridgeline.

One of the Keyowah warriors seemed to be staring straight out at the rebel yacht. At such a great distance, it was impossible to tell, but it was as if he was looking directly at the lieutenant. The warrior raised his rifle and steadied it.

The lieutenant smiled and shook his head. "How far out are we?" he asked.

A flash and a puff of smoke provided evidence that the Keyowah warrior had fired a single round.

Wahroo stirred from his malaise. "What?"

There was a soft chiming crash, and a hole appeared in the suddenly spiderwebbed window glass. The lieutenant's body flew backwards onto the map table, spraying blood onto the front of Wahroo's uniform. The monocular spun clear of the lieutenant's hand and smashed hard into Wahroo's face. He dropped to the floor with a frightened yelp. Frantic, he crawled to the wheel, jammed the boat into gear and spun it around to open ocean.

In the bay, only four Tavington yachts remained afloat, all damaged. One of the four was on fire. The Zodiacs continued their work of rescue and recovery. It was a scene straight out of a madman's nightmare. Billowing clouds of black smoke and the screams of the dying filled the air. Gunfire rang out as the Malay sharpshooters continued their deadly sniper assault on the last rebel boat. Debris and dead bodies littered the bay.

Alistair Tavington's yacht pulled into the dock, listing slightly to one side. A group of men had assembled on deck. Caleb and Kanna arrived, walking from the shore, both shirtless and bleeding from numerous cuts and scrapes. As they made their way toward the deck, two Keyowah warriors walked up the beach carrying John Horn's body. They stopped near Alistair Tavington's yacht and dumped the body onto the sand.

On the way up the ramp, Caleb paused. He stared at Horn's face for a long moment.

"Son of a bitch," Kanna said. "John Horn."

Caleb nodded, then continued on.

The knot of men on deck spread apart to allow Caleb in. He stepped between those assembled and stopped. In front of him, Samuel knelt beside the body of their father, Alistair Tavington.

Samuel looked up at Caleb's approach, face wet with tears.

For a long, long moment, Caleb simply stood, staring down at his brother and the body of his father. It was as if he didn't want to take the step that would confirm what he saw, as if by standing still, he could somehow change the reality of what was in front of him.

"Caleb," Samuel sobbed, and the spell was broken.

Caleb stepped slowly forward and knelt down next to his father's body, his eyes wide with shock and disbelief. He placed his hand on his father's chest.

On the far side of the deck, two of Alistair Tavington's Indonesian servants sobbed and wailed uncontrollably, beating their chests in their grief. The sound of their cries provided an eerie backdrop to the picture of two princes at the side of a dead king.

Caleb let out a long exhale, his eyes fixed on his father's face. Tears welled up briefly, but he squeezed them away. Steadying himself, he lifted his father's hand and removed the Tavington family ring.

"Gently, Caleb," Samuel begged and used his own hand to lay his father's arm back down.

Caleb slid the ring onto his finger and stood. The look on his face made it very clear that he was now bearing the weight of the world on his shoulders.

He turned and faced the crowd of men on deck, his face set in a mask of anger, his eyes like black holes.

Immediately, Kanna stepped forward, took Caleb's hand, bowed and kissed the ring. Slowly, a line formed and, one by one, every man on deck did the same, kissing the ring and bowing to the new lord of the Tavington House. It was a surreal scene. The crackling of flames, the smoke, the sound of gunfire, the cries of the wounded and the grieving, all conspired to lend a terrible dark weight to the proceedings. Caleb Tavington had become the Lord of the Archipelago on the day the world burned down.

Suddenly, he snapped his head around and looked at Kanna. "Freetown."

CHAPTER NINE

The Tavington section of Freetown was a shambles, homes and buildings on fire, bodies everywhere. The entire scene was chaos and death. Every single structure had been damaged, many destroyed outright. The madman's nightmare that had enveloped Sister Bay had spread to Freetown.

Rescue and firefighting efforts were underway, but the damage was so immense, most of it could not be saved. The sound of women and children crying rang loud, even in the crackling of the flames.

Caleb stood with Kanna, watching Tavington Freetown burn down to the ground. In the private docking area adjacent to the section, all of the Tavington yachts were on fire. The devastation was beyond belief.

A crowd had gathered from neighboring sections. Dozens of Freetown residents were rushing in to help with the firefighting efforts and to assist the wounded.

A man stepped out of the crowd and approached Caleb and Kanna. They saw him coming and turned. "Council," said the man. "One hour."

As the man walked away, Emma Wallace and her brother, Michael, ran up, joining the crowd. Emma's hand flew to her mouth in horror, her eyes wide with shock. Michael tore off his shirt and sprinted toward the damaged buildings.

Emma scanned the crowd, finding Caleb. Their eyes met through the chaos, and they stared at each other for a long, tortured moment. Then Emma started to move toward Caleb but stopped suddenly. Just enough for her to notice, Caleb shook his head no. Emma turned away, her eyes filling with tears.

For the next hour, Caleb and his men fought fires and tended to the wounded. As the time ticked slowly by, the number of cloth-covered bodies laid in the Archipelago sun grew until they were two dozen in number. The wailing of grieving mothers and wives continued.

Finally, it was time for the Council meeting.

Caleb, Samuel, Kanna, Masu and Passo walked down Freetown's main street. The Tavington group was tattered, cut and bruised from the morning attack, covered in blood, sweat and ash from rescue and firefighting efforts.

Samuel looked as if he could break down and cry at any moment. Beside him, Caleb's face seemed carved in stone.

Around his neck, Kanna wore a leather thong. Threaded through the thong were what appeared to be human ears.

Word of the Council meeting had spread throughout the township, and the street was lined with bystanders, three or four deep. Freetown was a cauldron of anger, confusion and anticipation.

The group moved at a slow but determined pace, their eyes fixed on a large stately building set far apart from the rest of the buildings at the end of the street. The large building was ringed by guards armed to the teeth with automatic shotguns and machine guns. It was almost comical, the amount of deadly hardware on display. The guards were so densely packed together that any firefight would have seen them stumbling over each other to find clear shooting lanes. Still, the effect was sobering, a show of such massive force that anyone, no matter how well armed or determined, would be forced to give careful consideration to their actions before approaching.

The Tavington men moved on without hesitation or hurry.

"Expectin' trouble," Kanna mused. He grabbed one of the ears on his necklace and turned it as if he was helping it hear his words. "Did you hear that, Horn?" Kanna continued, raising his voice. "Expectin' trouble."

Kanna barked out a laugh, his bloodshot eyes scanning the crowd of bystanders. By all appearances, he was teetering on the edge, ready to explode.

Out of the packed lines of onlookers, John Ellis, the head of the Ellis family, stepped out and joined Caleb's group, matching their steady pace. Ellis was in his early forties, whipcord lean and darkly tanned, his hands and face scarred from years of back-alley brawling.

Ellis stretched out his hand without breaking stride, and Caleb grasped it. The group continued walking.

"The sea that binds us, John," Caleb said, voice flat. "Nice to see a friendly face."

"The sea that binds us, Caleb. I can't even tell you how sorry I am—"

"For later, John," Caleb interjected. "There'll be time."

Ellis nodded. "I understand," he said.

Caleb looked over, assessing Ellis's expression. "Where are we?" he asked.

"The word's out about John Horn," Ellis explained. "Everyone knows he was there this mornin', but Black's been spinnin' it all day, talkin' to Council members. He's sayin' Horn wasn't a Wallace man as of a week ago. Caught him stealin', locked him up, but somehow he skipped out."

Kanna growled, deep in his throat. "Bullshit," he said, furious. "That won't wash." He grabbed an ear from his necklace and shouted into it. "Hear that, Horn? That bullshit won't wash."

Ellis eyed Kanna warily. "Already has," he said.

Caleb stopped walking and turned to look at Ellis. A little shiver ran through the nearby crowd.

Ellis sighed. "Council doesn't want a piece of Wallace, Caleb, and nobody in their right mind wants a piece of you. So, Council's deaf, dumb and blind for the duration."

"When you break with a man who knows the map book, John," Caleb responded, "you don't lock him up, you hang him…on the spot. That's the law."

"Council ain't splittin' hairs with Wallace right now, Caleb. They want to believe him."

"And the rebels?" Caleb asked. "They came through the gap at speed, John. No trial and error."

Ellis frowned, dumbfounded. "What are you sayin'?"

"He's saying they've got the goddamn reef," Kanna snarled. "He's saying Wallace gave the monkeys a map book."

The look on John Ellis's face was one of complete bewildered shock. "Wallace has already told Council that he can account for all of his books after Horn's breakout." He shook his head, looked around as if to see whether anyone nearby could hear their conversation. "You can't bring that, brother," he said, voice lowered. "Not without video and twenty eyewitnesses to back it up. It's too big…and Wallace will just say that Horn led 'em."

Caleb turned away and began walking again. "What about the attack itself?" he said. "What are they going to do about the rebels who did this?"

"Up in the air," Ellis replied. "They need to see the cards before they play their hand."

Caleb nodded, his face again set in a mask of stone.

The group continued their slow walk toward the heavily guarded building at the end of the street.

. . . .

The Freetown Council chamber was a solemn place, quiet and dimly lit, like a cathedral. Or a mausoleum. The floors were thickly carpeted, adding to the muted, solemn air. The hum of powerful air-conditioning provided constant noise-dampening. Footsteps were never heard, chairs didn't scrape along the floor. Every sound was hushed. Every movement occurred in silence.

This seat of power was as quiet as a graveyard.

The room itself was dominated by a long semicircular table. Twenty-one seats occupied spaces at that table, divided into seven groups of three, three seats for each of the seven Council families. Each group of three was separated from the others by a low glass barrier.

At the front of the room was a dais on which sat a grand desk and chair. Behind the desk, an old Malaysian man presided over Council in white judges' robes.

Today, the Council chamber was unusually crowded, packed with armed guards, a wall-to-wall sea of tension, bristling with automatic weapons. There were so many men that they were forced to turn sideways to accommodate all of the bodies and armaments. Every type of close- and medium-range weapon was visible: handguns, shotguns, short-barreled submachine guns, close-quarter semiautomatics, and even stun batons. The guards wore the colors of all the families, except for the Wallaces and

Tavingtons. They stood, silent and nervous, eyes locked on Caleb Tavington and Black Wallace, ready for the worst.

At the table, every seat had been taken by representatives of the seven families: Tavington, Ellis, Warwicke, Beauchamp, Kench, Smythe, and Wallace. Behind each group of three seats stood two family bodyguards.

The bodyguards flicked their eyes back and forth, knowing that trouble was coming.

Caleb, Kanna and Samuel sat at the Tavington section of the table. Masu and Passo stood guard behind them.

On the opposite side sat Black Wallace, Michael Wallace and Tanner.

Next to the Tavingtons were John Ellis and his family representatives.

The old Malaysian man cleared his throat.

"We recognize the lord of the Tavington House, Caleb," he began. "We extend our heartfelt condolences for the manner of his ascension. Alistair Tavington will be sorely missed. The hearts of this council are heavy with the loss."

A murmur of condolence came from those present. All eyes turned to Caleb. Instead of standing himself, Caleb nodded to Kanna, who moved to the front of the dais. Kanna stood, half facing the old man and half facing the table of families.

Into the tense silence, his voice rasped like steel on stone.

"As you know," he said, "Sister Bay was attacked this morning...and Freetown, by rebel cowards who murdered sleeping women and children. Rebel cowards"—at this, he held up the ears on his leather necklace and stared directly at Black Wallace—"and Wallace's man, John Horn."

A stir of recognition ran through the room. The Council members realized what Kanna was wearing around his neck.

The old man held up his hand for silence. "Warwicke," he said with a nod to a man at the table.

At his place, Lachlan Warwicke addressed Caleb. "Caleb, Eamon has satisfied Council that John Horn acted on his own initiative."

Caleb didn't even turn his head. He gave no indication that he had heard Warwicke at all. Instead, he nodded to Kanna to continue.

Kanna raised his voice as he spoke. "The rebel attack on the Tavington House is an attack on Council, and our response should be clear to all. Council is at war."

Some murmurings of assent came from the assemblage. Most members, however, sat quietly.

Black Wallace surveyed the room with a scowl. "Is it the Tavingtons who decide for us when this council goes to war?" he asked.

"We are under attack, Eamon," John Ellis responded.

Black sniffed with disdain. "Are we under attack, John?" He scanned the table. "Or are the Tavingtons under attack?"

"An assault on one is an assault on all."

"That's a pretty sentiment," Black said, "but the Tavingtons are an ambitious family with many business concerns. If some private issue has caused them difficulty with the rebels, is that Council business, or is that Tavington business?"

"They attacked Freetown, Eamon—"

"They didn't attack my goddamn Freetown, John, or yours for that matter." Black looked around the table. "Or any of yours," he continued. "The Tavington section was singled out. That doesn't seem like an attack on Council to me."

Black's words were having the desired effect on Council. The room was unsure. It was clearly evident in the faces of those assembled. Black's absolute confidence and intimidating presence combined to bulldoze his message through any objections that might have been forming.

Kanna's face was suffused with rage, the veins on his forehead writhing as he fixed Black Wallace with a murderous stare.

Unfazed by Kanna, Black continued.

"This assembly was not created to protect the Tavingtons...or any family. It exists to protect the reef, to enforce the code under which we all live: 'Knowledge of the reef is a sacred trust and must be defended at any and all cost.' It is not the business of this council to interfere in affairs that do not concern it."

Next to Wallace, his son, Michael, stared straight ahead. He didn't appear to be paying attention to any of the proceedings around him. His lips moved soundlessly, as if he was talking to himself.

Caleb rested his eyes on Michael for a few moments.

From across the table, Warwicke raised his voice. "Are you suggesting we ignore the rebel attack, Eamon?"

Black shook his head. "Of course not," he said. "We must be ever vigilant in the Archipelago. But for all we know, this is some private contention between Caleb's Malaysian friends and the rebels. Are we to be sucked into that? Will we sacrifice good men, good white men, in a mutt war?"

Caleb smoldered, his eyes hard. He looked around at the Council members, and it was clear that they were eager to believe Black. A few of the families had begun whispered conversations, and Caleb gritted his teeth as he watched the head-nodding among them.

Finally, he spoke. "What is the going rate for an XR-17 blockade runner?" he asked, voice carrying over the hum of whispered discussions.

"What?" Warwicke responded.

"Fully loaded," Caleb said. "The going rate?"

Warwicke considered for a moment. "Almost three million dollars," he said. "With deck guns, armor...and radar."

"How is it that the rebels can afford boats like that?" Caleb allowed his eyes to sweep over the table as he asked his question.

Raillie Smythe, the head of the Smythe family, answered. "They cannot."

Caleb nodded. "Last week," he said, "the Indonesian government seized an XR-17 from the rebel base at Lano. I saw it."

This caused a great disturbance in the room. The intensity that had been missing in the assemblage suddenly made an appearance. The old man was forced to raise his arm for silence.

Caleb fixed on Black Wallace. "If the rebels cannot afford boats like that," he said, "then they must have found a friend who can."

All eyes riveted on the confrontation. Every person in the room had known that this meeting would ultimately come down to the Wallace and Tavington families pitted against each other.

The wall-to-wall armed guards stood tense and ready.

"Caleb..." Warwicke spoke with a tone of warning.

Black Wallace smiled. "Young Tavington has made my point for me. The rebels must have indeed found a benefactor if they possess boats like the XR-17. And who might that benefactor be?"

He paused for effect.

"We all know that the Tavingtons have powerful business associates, men whose very names command influence on a global scale, multibillionaires who control cartels and syndicates...and even governments. These men rule the world. We know who they are, we know what they are capable of, and we know that the Tavingtons are in bed with them. Do we not?"

Black could sense that he had the room wavering, unsure. One small push was all he needed to gain the advantage.

"And what if the Tavingtons have had a...difficulty...with one of these men?" he asked. "What if they have fallen out with someone like...Vajani Singh? Or Ira Salisbury? Or even Solomon? These men pick up the phone and call presidents, if they choose. It would be nothing for them to buy an XR-17, or a dozen, or even fifty, for the rebel army."

With these words, Black Wallace could see that he had moved Council to his side of the equation. The Tavington family's connections with powerful global interests were enough to throw doubt into their minds.

Caleb could feel the shift in Council as well. The status quo had presented itself as the best option. He had known that the men around the table would choose a false peace over anything else.

Kanna's patience, such as it was, had run out. With a growl, he tore the leather thong off his neck and hurled John Horn's ears at Black Wallace.

"Challenge," he screamed.

Suddenly, there were weapons everywhere, out and pointed, along with shouted threats overriding the few calls for calm. Every single person, except for the actual family heads, was aiming a weapon at somebody. The room was in a total standoff. Any wrong move would have seen a bloodbath.

Still, the heads of the families were calm, and deliberately so. Eventually the shouting died down. Only the high-wire tension remained.

"Challenge is not recognized in Council, Kanna," Warwicke said in a loud, clear voice. "You know that."

Kanna's face was a gargoyle mask of tattoos and rage. "Hell with you, Warwicke," he spat, "and hell with Council."

At his place, Caleb drummed his fingers on the table. The sound drew Kanna's attention, and he stepped back with a deep breath.

Caleb stood, and there was a shadow of menace about him, the promise of sudden violence. He was different, somehow, than everyone else, heavier, darker. It was etched into every movement he made, and the assembled families were well aware of the danger. They knew the stories, the terrible legends of bloodshed and mystery, and it was enough to ensure that Caleb Tavington was respected and feared.

Caleb walked around the side of the table and made his way slowly toward the Wallace seats. He stopped with less than six feet separating him from Black Wallace. A ripple of anticipation swept along the crowd of armed guards.

"Many of mine are dead today, Black," he said, his voice flat.

"Life can be hard that way," Black Wallace responded.

Caleb nodded. His eyes were like black holes, pinpricks of darkness. "Yes, it can," he said. "But I am steadfast, and patient...and God is watching you."

Black Wallace placed his hands on the table in front of him and pushed himself slowly to his feet. "Today has been very hard for you, young Tavington, and you've said a thing or two that could be misinterpreted...as accusations." Black shrugged and shook his head. "I don't hold it against you. Not while you're under such duress."

Black gestured to his men, and they stood as one, except for Michael, who didn't appear to be tracking the proceedings. Tanner tapped him on the shoulder and helped him to his feet.

"Perhaps," Black continued, "it would be best if we stepped out. It seems that speaking the plain truth has made me the target of Tavington anger." Black held Caleb's stare for a long moment, then turned and started up the aisle to the exit.

As he watched them go, Caleb noticed a spot of blood on Tanner's shirt. "Hurt yourself, Tan?" he asked.

Tanner looked back but didn't respond. He and the others followed Black Wallace out of the Council chamber.

When the doors closed behind the Wallace party, Caleb turned to face the Council. "My father believed in this Council," he said. "He believed that, together, the seven families could keep the peace in the Archipelago." Caleb took a few moments and scanned the table, meeting the eyes of every single family head, one after the other. "He was wrong."

Caleb's voice hardened. "If you cannot find the courage to act now, you never will. But understand this. Precious Tavington blood was spilled today and I...will...never...rest. Alistair Tavington was a good man, a better man than all of you. He will be avenged. If the islands of the Archipelago and the streets of Freetown must run red with blood, he will be avenged."

When Caleb finished speaking, there was complete silence in the chamber. Nobody moved or made a sound. Caleb walked back to his seat, joined by Kanna, who glared at the assembly as he went.

Once Caleb was seated and it was clear there would be nothing more from the Tavingtons, Warwicke stood. "We are adjourned," he announced.

The Council members filed out quietly, as if worried that sound might provoke Caleb somehow. Kanna watched them with a look of disdain.

Within a few minutes, the chamber was empty, save for the Tavington group and John Ellis. Ellis walked over and stood in front of Caleb.

Caleb gave Ellis a grim smile. "Thank you for standing for me, John," he said.

Ellis responded with a nod, his face somber.

Caleb took a deep breath, then motioned to Kanna and the others. "Get ready to get out," he ordered. "I'll be along. Sam, you're with them."

Samuel didn't react to the sound of his name. He stared blankly at the far wall. Kanna shook him gently and helped him to his feet, then guided him along the aisle and out the chamber exit.

"What will you do, Caleb?" Ellis asked.

"I'm moving. To Seti Bay. Sister Bay is soft now. Too hard to defend."

"Seti's a good spot," Ellis said with an approving nod. "Good water all around."

"And I'm going after them at Katalo, John. Tomorrow."

Ellis's face showed his surprise at hearing this. "Katalo's bloody hard, Caleb," he said. "If you step wrong, that'll be the shittiest place on earth."

Caleb grimaced. "I have no choice," he responded. "I'm too thin...if I wait for them to come to me, I won't have a chance. I need to hit them where they live."

"Are you sure they'd come for you again?"

"They'll come," Caleb said, and there was a tone of certainty in his voice. "Black will make sure of it. They have the reef, John. Without it, we're all just like any flea-bitten ragtag pirates that hug coastlines anywhere in Asia."

Caleb rubbed his eyes. "Without the reef," he went on, "nothing protects us...it's open season. If I don't take them out now, I never will. Hell is waiting, John, and without the reef, I'll see it sooner than I thought."

A heavy silence descended between the two men. Ellis offered no argument to what Caleb had just said. It was obvious by the look on his face that he agreed.

"I'm sorry about your da, Caleb," he said in a whisper. "I really am. He was a man among men, and a good friend."

Caleb held out his hand. "Thank you, John."

Ellis shook the proffered hand with fitting solemnity. "Fight well, Caleb boy," he said, then turned and walked to the exit, leaving Caleb alone in the empty Council chamber. As the door closed behind Ellis, Caleb's eyes focused on the Wallace section of the table. In total silence he sat, eyes fixed on Black Wallace's seat.

Finally, he shook his head, stood, and walked out of the Council chamber into the streets of Freetown.

· · · ·

In the early afternoon, the back room at Lord Nelson's Saloon was empty and dark, with Caleb the only patron and one black-coated servant nearby. Caleb sat at the table he and his father had occupied the night before.

He heard a sound and turned.

In the doorway stood Emma, tears in her eyes. Her face was stricken, lips trembling.

Caleb pushed his chair back slowly and rose as Emma ran toward him. With a last glance at the chair opposite him, he pulled her hard into his arms.

"Oh, Caleb," Emma whispered with a sob. "It's just not possible that he's gone. He was so…I can't believe—"

"I know," Caleb said.

Emma buried her face in his chest, crying. "I'm so sorry," she gasped.

They stood like that for a few long moments, frozen in the tinted Archipelago sunlight from Alistair Tavington's picture windows, holding each other tight.

Finally, Caleb took Emma's tear-stained face in his hands. "I'm sorry too, Em."

Emma smiled sadly, understanding. She stared out at the ocean on the horizon. "It was just a dream, Caleb," she said. "A beautiful dream…and it disappeared with the dawn, like all dreams." Her voice broke. "You were right. The Archipelago always wins."

Caleb responded in a dull monotone. "She gives and she takes…and takes."

Emma shut her eyes hard, squeezing out the tears.

"How did you find me?" Caleb asked.

"This was where you saw him last in Freetown," Emma answered. "I knew you would be here."

Caleb considered Emma's words for a moment, then glanced around, checking the servant's position and the door. Emma noticed. "Yes." She nodded. "You should go."

Suddenly, she pulled Caleb's face down into a violent, almost desperate kiss. "I'm coming with you, Caleb," she said in a fierce whisper. "It doesn't matter now. If they are killing Tavingtons, I want to be with you."

Caleb shook his head. "Soon, Em, but it's too dangerous right now. I'm at Seti Bay. Soon. When the water's right, I'll come for you."

Emma took a deep, ragged breath and wiped the tears from her eyes. "Do what you must do, Caleb," she said, "and don't worry about me. I will wait for you. I will always wait for you."

• • • •

The main dock at Freetown was abuzz with activity. Tavington men loaded supplies and weapons onto three ready ships and numerous smaller craft while dozens of armed guards blocked access from the shoreline. The Archipelago sun shone down, hot and bright, as the Tavington family prepared to abandon the township and relocate to the more defensible Seti Bay.

A long whistle sounded, and the ramp connecting to Caleb's yacht to the dock detached itself with a loud metallic grind. Caleb, Kanna and Samuel stood at the deck rail, facing Freetown, as the ship's engines hummed to life.

On the dock, Luke raised his right arm in a half-salute, which Caleb returned, and the yacht pulled away, motoring toward open ocean.

Kanna shook his head. "Mother of Jesus," he said in a barely audible voice. "It's hard to believe. Two hundred years, and now they've got the reef. Goddamn Wallace to hell."

Beside him, Samuel leaned against the deck rail as if, without the support, he would simply collapse. His weary eyes stared back at the smoke still drifting up from the Tavington section of

Freetown. With a sound like a sob, he turned away and walked to the stairwell.

CHAPTER TEN

Samuel's cabin was dark, thick drapes over the porthole windows blocking the fading Archipelago sun. In the rumpled bed, Samuel slept, still in his clothes, his body twisted in the sheets. He jerked and mumbled, gripped in some hellish dream, his face torn by grief and fear.

A pounding sounded on the door. Samuel stopped moving. The pounding came again, and this time he sat up. Panicked, he fumbled for the light, ripping off his eye shades as he did so.

"W-what is it?" he croaked, groggy.

Passo threw the door open. "Up hard, Sam," he ordered, all business. "Trouble comin.'"

He turned to go but stopped suddenly, staring at Samuel's hands.

"I know you're fresh back, boy," he said, "but you're in the Archipelago, now. Someone pounds your door like I just did, you better roll out with more than your dick in your hand."

Samuel nodded, still disoriented. "I-I don't have a gun, Passo," he stuttered.

Passo turned and ran down the hall. "Top drawer of your bedside table, Sammy," he yelled over his shoulder. "Double-time it. Your brother's waiting."

Samuel opened the drawer and pulled out a pistol. He stared at it for a long moment, then dropped his head and rubbed his eyes.

Moments later, he stumbled into the map room on the bridge—disheveled, eyes bloodshot, holding his pistol by the barrel, like a hammer.

Caleb, Kanna and Passo sat at the map table, in heavy discussion. Masu occupied a chair just adjacent, cleaning a pistol carefully, cigarette dangling from his lips. All looked up at Samuel's entrance.

"What's going on?" Samuel asked, breathing heavily.

"Tuck your shirt in and have a seat, Sam," Caleb responded.

Samuel straightened himself out, pointing the pistol at everyone in the room in the process. Caleb gave Kanna a look. Kanna stood up and gently took the pistol out of Samuel's hand.

"Let me hang on to this for you, boyo," he offered. "Before you circumcise yourself."

Samuel smiled, embarrassed, and sat down.

"Do you remember Vakona, Sam?" Caleb asked.

"Vakona, the village? Yeah. They fish for us."

"That's right." Caleb nodded. "They fish for us and we protect them...from monsters."

Samuel looked around the table. He took a deep breath. "So," he said, "we've got monsters?"

"We've got monsters," Kanna replied in a grim voice. "The word is out. The ragtags smell blood...our blood, and they're checking to see how soft we really are."

"And we're too damn soft to ignore it," Caleb added. "If we blink, there are hundreds of small-timers waiting, and they will overrun every village under our protection."

Samuel squeezed his eyes shut, then exhaled and opened them again. "I'm ready."

. . . .

The Vakona village saloon was a simple affair: one long bar on the wall by the door, scattered tables under hanging lights, wood-shuttered windows on the front and back walls and a rear exit door under a second floor balcony.

On this particular evening, the saloon was almost full, but not with customers. Rather, the people who crowded against the walls, sobbing and afraid, were prisoners and hostages.

At the bar stood seven heavily armed Indonesian pirates, the same greasy lot who had looted the millionaire vacationers' yacht. Their leader, Copsa, leaned against the counter, ugly face even uglier from Caleb's beating.

In front of Copsa, two Vakona villagers knelt, bound and gagged, faces bloody. Against the far wall, a large group of villagers huddled together near overturned tables.

Footsteps sounded from the boards outside the swinging-door entryway.

Copsa straightened.

Through the doors pushed Caleb, with Masu just behind. They stood side by side in the entryway, surveying the scene, soaking wet, puddles of water forming at their feet.

Copsa gave the rapidly expanding puddles and wet clothing a pointed look and smiled. "Humid tonight," he said, thick accent even thicker through swollen lips.

Caleb nodded. With both hands, he wrung out the front of his shirt, splashing water on the floor in front of him.

"From the beach just outside this village," he said, "the sunset is always dark red, like blood. No one knows why, but it's really quite beautiful." Caleb took a moment to look all the Indonesians in the face. "Just thought you should know," he continued, "since none of you will live to see it."

The rear door opened and three of Caleb's men sauntered in, blood spattered on their hands and clothing. One of them wiped blood off a wicked-looking blade as he walked. They spread out casually, facing the ragged bunch at the bar.

Caleb met Copsa's eyes. "Oh, by the way...your ship's on fire."

Copsa walked to one of the windows near the end of the bar and opened the wooden shutters. On the water, his pirate ship was engulfed in flames. Two bodies hung from the bow rail.

Copsa watched his ship burn for a few moments, then closed the shutters and faced Caleb again. His glance flickered to the second-floor balcony.

Caleb allowed his eyes to follow Copsa's, moving to the balcony as well. "Don't get your hopes up," he said, shaking his head.

Kanna appeared at the balcony rail, holding a bloody knife, which he dangled from his fingers, blade down. He winked at Copsa and blew him a kiss.

Copsa clenched his jaws.

Masu took a small step forward and spoke, in Bahasa Indonesia, to Copsa. "Time to die."

Kanna let the knife drop. All eyes watched as the blade fell fifteen feet from the balcony to the floor below.

Suddenly, Copsa's hand blurred to a pistol in his waist sash. He drew it quickly, snapping off two wild shots, one into the floor and one into the doorjamb near Caleb.

Caleb and his men reacted like lightning, exploding into action, guns out and blazing. The Indonesian pirates were caught flat-footed, unprepared for their leader's sudden move. They attempted to return fire, but their slow response was fatal, and they were mowed down under the barrage of Tavington bullets.

The firefight was brief and bloody. When the shooting stopped, all of the Indonesian pirates were down, dead or dying, shot to rag dolls.

One of Caleb's men was dead and one wounded—writhing in agony on the floor. Two of the Vakona villagers were also dead.

Caleb surveyed the damage, eyes cold. He walked forward and squatted coolie-style beside Copsa, the pirate leader still alive, eyes blinking, blood flecking his lips. Copsa half smiled and tried to speak, coughing through the blood.

Caleb leaned down. "You weren't enough," he whispered. "Tell God. You weren't enough. None of us are. It's not your fault."

At that moment, Samuel entered and stopped short, blanching at the carnage. He looked as if he could be sick at any moment.

Caleb lifted his head. "Sam. Come here," he ordered. Caleb dragged Copsa to his feet and forced him to stand. Samuel walked up, face pale. "Kanna, give Sam his gun back."

Kanna clenched his jaws and stared at Caleb for a long moment. Finally, he stepped forward and handed a confused Samuel the gun he had taken from him earlier.

"Sam," Caleb said, "this man is our enemy. Tonight, he spilled Tavington blood. You're going to kill him."

Samuel took a quick step backward. He blinked his eyes.

"He tried to steal what is ours, Sam. Only God can take what belongs to the Tavington family."

Caleb stepped away, leaving Copsa to stand on his own. The pirate leader understood what was happening. He straightened, eyes proud, ready to die.

Samuel shook his head. "Caleb," he said, voice shaking. "I-I don't think that—"

"Talk is for lawyers, Sam," Caleb cut him off, his voice cold. "You're not at Harvard now. Kill him. This is what Tavington justice feels like."

Samuel forced himself to point the pistol at Copsa. His hand shook. Beads of sweat broke out on his forehead.

Copsa stepped forward arrogantly, leaving a trail of blood behind him.

"Kill him, Sam," Caleb repeated. "Your family's honor requires it."

Samuel swallowed hard.

Copsa shuffled forward another step.

"Caleb, I—" Samuel began.

Copsa's hand flashed suddenly to his waist and he lunged at Samuel, a tiny dagger in his fist.

A gunshot rang out. Copsa crumpled to the floor.

Samuel was frozen, pistol still extended. He looked behind him, and Kanna was there, smoking gun in his hand.

Caleb stared down at the dead Copsa, then back up at Samuel. Under his brother's glare, Samuel wilted. He dropped his head and walked out of the saloon.

• • • •

On the beach just outside Vakona village, Samuel stood near the water's edge, watching the sunset. It was just as Caleb had described it. Blood red. Fingers of deep crimson and purpling scarlet twisted across the horizon in an otherworldly burst of color. It was as if the sky was bleeding out.

Beside Samuel, Caleb stood with his back to the sunset, facing toward the village. The sound of hammering echoed in the evening quiet, striking and loud against the gentle lapping of the waves.

"Do you ever get afraid, Caleb?" Samuel asked, his voice small.

"Since I was fifteen years old," Caleb answered. "I've been afraid every day of my life."

"I don't believe that. You always know exactly what to do." Samuel shook his head. "I never know."

Caleb pressed his lips into a thin, hard line. He considered Samuel's words as the hammers continued their rhythm.

"We have no country, Sam," he finally said. "We bend our knee to no earthly power. Your only enduring obligation is to ensure that, at the end of the day, Tavington colors fly over Tavington water. Every decision you make...every choice...must best serve Tavington interests."

"What if you choose wrong?"

Caleb smiled. "Every morning," he said, "my men wake up and place their lives in my hands...and every single morning I wake up wondering if today is the day that I get them all killed. If I choose wrong, then today is that day."

The hammering stopped.

Caleb turned his head to look at Samuel. "Turn around, Sam. Taste the Archipelago."

Sam hesitated, then turned slowly.

Lined up on the beach stood ten large wooden crosses. On each cross hung the body of an Indonesian pirate, crucified, hands and feet nailed to the wood. The ten crosses faced the ocean, a grisly warning to all who passed by this beach.

Samuel dropped to his knees and vomited loudly. "I-I'm...trying my best, Caleb," he whispered, gasping for air.

Caleb stared down at his brother. "I know you are," he said and put his hand on Samuel's shoulder. "It's all you'll ever need to do. It's all I'll ever ask of you."

CHAPTER ELEVEN

In the conference room of the Wallace yacht, Michael sat alone at the bar, eyes bloodshot and glossy with tears of self-pity. He poured a glass from a bottle of whiskey that was already half-empty. A white-coated servant stood nearby, the only one present to hear Michael's mumbling and incoherent sobbing. The young Wallace was the picture of a man completely broken.

He checked his watch and lifted his red-rimmed eyes to the windows lining one wall of the conference room. With a groan, he pushed himself to his feet.

Minutes later, Emma Wallace walked along the hallway toward her cabin, past the conference room so recently occupied by her brother. She was stooped from exhaustion, on the verge of collapse after a long day helping the injured at Freetown. She glanced into the room as she went, spotting the almost-empty bottle of whiskey at the bar. With a sad shake of her head, she continued on along the hallway.

Passing an open door to the deck, Emma stopped suddenly, surprised. Outside, a disheveled, miserable-looking Michael was escorting Caleb's cousin, Luke, up the gangplank.

Emma stepped outside. "Luke?" she said.

Luke stepped back, startled. "Wha—?!" He let out a bark of laughter. "Jesus, Em. You scared the hell out of me."

A look of worry crept onto Emma's face. "Luke, what are you doing here? What's happened? Why...?"

Emma glanced at Michael, who simply stared at the horizon with groggy eyes.

Luke held up his hands in a calming gesture.

"Easy now, girl," he said, "I'm just passin' through. Things got a little out of hand at Council today and Caleb wanted me to talk to your da...see if we could sort this thing out...without getting everybody killed."

"How is Caleb?" Emma asked, trying to keep her voice neutral.

"Caleb?" Luke shrugged. "He's...Caleb. Took his father's death pretty hard and said some things he shouldn't have. But he's cooled off and doesn't want this to get any worse. Now, get some sleep, darlin'. You look like you could use it."

Luke winked, grabbed Emma and gently turned her around. "We appreciated what you did at Freetown today," he added. "We could have used a few more like you. Now, off to sleep, before you fall over." Luke eased her on her way with a soft guiding pat toward the door.

Once Emma had disappeared into the ship, Luke turned to Michael. "Your sister's quite a woman," he said.

Michael didn't respond. His bloodshot eyes stared blankly into Luke's face. Finally, he inclined his head toward the bridge, and Luke started walking again.

· · · ·

On the bridge, Black Wallace sipped a glass of whiskey at the map table. A knock on the door drew his attention.

"Come," he said.

Luke entered and looked around the room carefully, as if searching out the shadows for an ambush. He took two steps forward and stopped, facing Black.

"Your son seems upset, Eamon," he said, watching Black's face carefully. "Something bothering him?"

Black waved his hand in a dismissive gesture. "He's at that age, Luke. Everything's tragic. Have a seat."

Luke nodded. He took another step forward and pulled back a chair, then eased himself into it.

Michael remained at the door, eyes downcast. While Luke and his father exchanged their greetings, he moved back into the hallway and pulled the door shut.

For long minutes, he simply stood, showing no interest at all in the conversation taking place on the other side of the door. His lips moved soundlessly, and every now and then, he shook his head, as if he was arguing with himself.

Finally, the meeting was over, and Luke opened the door.

Michael spun, unsteady on his feet, and led the way back toward the gangplank.

As they emerged from the stairwell onto the main deck, Tanner stepped out of the nearby shadows, smoking a cigarette.

Luke gave Tanner a long look. "Those'll kill you," he said.

Tanner took a long pull on the cigarette and spoke through a cloud of smoke. "Don't be a stranger."

Luke laughed and walked down the gangplank.

Tanner watched him go, then turned to Michael. "Go to bed, boy," he said. "You look like shit. I'll take over."

Michael seemed not to have heard Tanner. He swayed slightly, staring into the darkness surrounding the dock.

Tanner finished his cigarette in silence, eyes alert.

A movement in the darkness drew both men's attention. Soon, a figure materialized and walked along the dock toward the gangplank. It was Captain Wahroo.

Michael sighed, pushed himself from the rail and walked away.

• • • •

Minutes later, Tanner stuck his head into the map room, where Black Wallace remained, glass of whiskey still in hand.

"Your guest is here," Tanner said.

Black nodded, and Tanner's head disappeared, to be replaced by Wahroo. The captain closed the door behind him and walked to the map table. Black watched him come, glowering.

"You've been quite a disappointment thus far," he said, his voice low and thick with anger.

Wahroo nodded. His eyes shifted back and forth, as if he couldn't find a safe place to look. "Tavington's action was...unexpected."

The captain's voice sounded soft and indistinct, lacking conviction.

"Unexpected?" Black snorted his contempt. "You waited too long, goddamnit. Caleb Tavington will eat your monkey heart, and that might be a little 'unexpected' too."

Wahroo made a visible effort to rally. "Alistair Tavington is dead, is he not? That is something."

Black's jaws clenched in barely suppressed anger. There was a wildness in his eyes, something unnatural and dark.

"You mutts have a short memory," he growled. "Do I need to remind you who this is? This is Caleb Tavington. Ask the Pawan tribe who he is..." Black tilted his head and leaned forward, like a predator poised to strike. "But you can't, can you? Because he didn't leave any of them alive...not a man, woman or child."

Wahroo pulled a chair back from the table.

"Don't sit," Black said. "You're not staying." He downed the remaining whiskey in his glass. "Do you believe in God, Captain?"

Wahroo nodded.

"Good." Black's dropped to a low growl. "Because only God...and I...can save you now."

• • • •

In her cabin, Emma sat on the bed, freshly showered and changed, holding the photograph of her and Caleb as children, in the kayak. Tears burgeoned in her eyes, then rolled down her face. She wiped them away and stood suddenly, as if something had just pulled her to her feet. A look of resolve replaced the sadness.

Minutes later, she was on deck, lowering a Zodiac into the ocean. She turned the crank as quickly as she could, but in her haste, her hands slipped several times off the handle. A sound behind her made her turn.

Black Wallace and Tanner stood watching her, amused, with another Wallace man, Clay Abelard, just behind them.

"Late for a Zodiac ride, isn't it, darlin' girl?" Black asked innocently.

Emma gave her father a flat stare. "I have something important to do," she said.

"Something important?" Black said, sounding appropriately impressed. "Well, maybe I could have Clay help you with it, whatever it is. He's all rested up and fresh, just off a lovely vacation in Malaysia. Beautiful little resort island."

Clay nodded, a greasy smile on his face. "Gorgeous place," he sneered. "Photographer's dream, really. I snapped a bunch of good ones. Wish I coulda stayed longer."

Emma stared, stunned, from Clay to Tanner to her father. All three men reflected her stare with open faces, as if they were simply having a pleasant conversation.

"You know," Black said, "I'd rather you stayed on board for a little while. It's not safe right now. Devilish things going on in the Archipelago, things that shouldn't be going on."

Emma couldn't keep the disgust off her face. She let go of the crank.

Black smiled. "Tanner, see that she gets safely to her room." He winked at Emma. "Just can't be too careful, darlin'. Hard to know who you can trust anymore. Tanner'll take care of you."

Black Wallace and Clay walked away, leaving Tanner with Emma.

"What if I decide I don't want to stay?" she asked, her voice shaking with anger.

Tanner shrugged. "Don't make this hard, Em," he said. "I don't have a choice. One way or another, you're staying."

"Are you going to put your hands on me, Tan?"

"Just come along easy, girl. It's better this way. Things are going to get shitty around here."

Emma looked out at the open ocean, then back at Tanner. She stood tall, brushed past him, and made her way to her cabin.

· · · ·

Far away from the Wallace yacht, the cliffs at Seti Bay stood sheer and sharp, vertical walls of rock, thrust from the ocean into the sky by an undersea volcano, now centuries dormant. For decades, the bay had served as the second home of the Tavington family, its sheltered water able to withstand any storm. Seti Bay and the island that held it had never been breached, protected on all sides by a solid razor reef. The navigation gaps cut into that reef were narrow and winding, and many were false, leading would-be invaders into a dead end from which no ship could escape. Seti Bay was impossible to conquer. No one had even made the attempt in more than a hundred years.

Tonight, the cliffs were alive with activity. Torches and lanterns lined the edge facing the bay, and Tavington men built watchtowers, sniper bunkers and sheltering huts. Fortifications were being erected to protect the island and the bay from all directions. Heavy gunners lay in their positions, stockpiling ammunition for a siege.

Just off the lighted edge of the main promontory, Caleb and his men sat at a map table under a pavilion tent. Lanterns hung from all corners of the tent, providing light to the assembly. The men were bone-tired, worn to threads by the trauma of the day, all of them still bearing the smears of ash and blood from the morning's battle and the Freetown fire.

Three white-coated servants attended them, serving tea and pastries on china and silver. It presented an incongruous picture, the struggle-weary soldiers taking refreshment as if it was high tea in an English garden.

Below them, several yachts bobbed up and down to the rhythm of the bay's sheltered currents. Preparations were underway there as well, Tavington men arming and armoring the ships. Bonfires burned on shore, casting eerie shadows across the water. Outside of the reef, smaller intercept boats patrolled the ocean in every direction. Heavily armed men guarded the cliffs and shoreline.

Under the canopy, Samuel turned to Caleb. "Do we have enough, Caleb?" he asked in a tired whisper. "To attack their base? Do we even know where it is?"

Kanna answered. "It's the last thing they'll be expecting, Sammy. They know we're swimmin' in shit. An attack from us is the one thing that they won't be ready for."

Samuel stared out at the night, at all of the activity in the bay. He looked like a zombie. "You were born in this bay, weren't you, Caleb? And Father."

Caleb gave Samuel an assessing look. "Get some sleep, Sam," he said. "Tomorrow will be hard."

Samuel gave a tired laugh, his face completely expressionless. He was a man on autopilot. "Today was hard, Caleb," he said. "Tomorrow will just be tomorrow."

Kanna watched Samuel, concerned. Even Caleb gave the moment proper pause. He was, after all, familiar with the dark. There was damage coming, he could tell, and the look on his face said that there was nothing he could do for his brother right now.

Samuel got up, steadied himself, then walked out into the night.

Caleb watched until Samuel could no longer be seen. Still he stared, eyes fixed on the darkness and whatever was waiting beyond it. "Pray for rain, gentlemen," he said. "It'll make us invisible...pray for rain."

• • • •

Back on the Wallace yacht, all was quiet and dark.

Below deck, Michael Wallace stood in front of his wardrobe mirror, breaking down, an almost-empty bottle in hand. He sobbed, mumbling to himself, and the look he gave his reflection was one of utter contempt. With a scream, he hurled the bottle, shattering the mirror. Shards of glass exploded out into the room and Michael lost his balance, toppling onto the floor in a disjointed heap.

For a moment, the heap lay still and then began a slow, pathetic crawl, through broken glass, toward the door.

Minutes later, a bleeding Michael stumbled down the hallway leading to Emma's cabin. A seated guard looked up, then stood to attention. Michael waved him back into his seat and motioned for him to open the door. The guard knocked on the door, then unlocked a large padlock.

Emma's voice sounded from inside the room. "Leave me alone," she said.

"It's me, Em," Michael responded. "It's Michael."

The door opened. Emma looked out, and her eyes widened when she saw Michael's appearance. She stepped back.

Michael walked into the room and closed the door behind him. Emma watched him sway for a moment, then disappeared into the bathroom and returned with a wet towel. She began treating the lacerations on his face, then his hands. All the while, he sat in silence, staring at the floor. Finally, he spoke.

"I'm going to do it, Em."

"Do what?" Emma asked.

"I'm going to kill him. I've promised myself...for years...kept myself alive with the hope that—"

"Michael," Emma said, resting her hand on Michael's cheek.

"Every time he knocked me down...every time he ridiculed me, I swore—"

"Michael," Emma said again, more firmly.

"He's gone too far, Em," Michael mumbled on, oblivious to Emma's interruptions. "He had no right..."

Emma lifted Michael's chin. Michael stopped talking. "I'm in love with Caleb," Emma said.

Michael jerked as if he had been slapped. He stared at Emma for a long moment, then dropped his head. "Oh God, Emma...oh my God."

Emma put her hand on his head.

Michael spoke again, his voice muffled. "Clay told me you were dropping a Zodiac. Is that where you were going...to Caleb?"

"Yes."

Michael took a deep, ragged breath. "It's in the water now, Em."

"What?"

"It's in the water. I just put it there."

Emma stood back. "Why?" she asked, in disbelief.

Michael smiled sadly. "Because I love you, Em...and I hate him."

Michael's eyes fell onto a photograph on Emma's table. It was the photo of him with Caleb, Emma and Samuel in a kayak. He picked it up with a trembling hand and a look of absolute despair as he recognized his own innocent, smiling face.

"Jesus, Em," he moaned, anguished. "What in God's name happened to me? I-I wanted to be so much...so much more. Where did this...person...go?"

Emma cupped Michael's face in her hands. "Shhh," she whispered, tears in her eyes. "It's not your fault. God cursed us both with a father who's a bastard."

Michael shut his eyes hard. "I just wish—"

"I know," Emma said, her voice breaking with emotion. "It's not your fault."

Michael shook himself, then stood. Emma stepped away, allowing him his path to the door.

"Please get some rest, Michael," she pleaded, but there was no real hope in her voice that her brother would listen.

Michael opened the door and paused. "I'm going to do it, Em. I'm going to kill him," he said, eyes flat. Michael closed the door behind him.

Emma walked slowly to the window and looked out. She stared into the Archipelago night, watching the moon's reflection on the water.

"If we wait," she whispered, echoing the words Caleb had spoken to her, "the Archipelago will win...and we'll be waiting forever." With a deep breath, she turned, strode to the door, and knocked.

Outside in the hallway, the guard snapped to alertness. He stood, unsure, his hand on his gun, and unlocked the door. "Yes?" he ventured.

Emma opened the door and stepped out into the hallway, forcing the man to take an involuntary step back. "I'm leaving now," she said in a matter-of-fact voice.

The guard started to draw his gun. Without a moment of hesitation, Emma pushed him against the wall, slapped him twice hard, and deftly slipped the gun out of his waistband. She pointed the weapon at his head and cocked the hammer back.

"You're new," she said. "What's your name?"

The stunned guard could barely speak. "R-Reuel," he finally managed.

"Okay, Reuel," Emma replied, "this is what's going to happen now. I'm leaving, and there is nothing you can do to stop me. When I'm gone, you have two choices. You can raise the alarm, tell my father I'm gone and then you'll be hanged. Or, you can sit quietly, guarding my door, and, sometime later tonight, leave unnoticed for a permanent vacation. Malaysia's nice this time of year. You decide."

Emma backed away down the hall. She gestured with the gun for Reuel to sit back down in his chair. Reuel did, dropping as if he was a puppet with his strings cut. After a few moments, he reached over and locked the door.

Emma smiled. "I usually have tea in an hour," she told him. "The galley will be expecting you to pick it up. Right after that would be a good time for you to leave."

So saying, Emma spun and ran through an exit door.

CHAPTER TWELVE

It was the hour before dawn, the darkest hour. The coldest hour. The moon glimmered on an ocean of solid black, sifting through a ghostly mist on the surface of Seti Bay. Four Tavington yachts motored slowly out of the bay, through the reef and toward the open ocean.

Caleb stood at the bridge rail of the lead yacht, staring through the glass window at the reflected light snaking toward the horizon. Behind him, Masu smoked a cigarette in the darkness.

On the main deck, the entire crew of Tavington men knelt, facing the bow, where a Catholic priest from St. Brendan's celebrated mass. It was an eerie scene: the cadence of the priest's voice, the moonlit deck and kneeling men, the hum of the engine swallowed by the vast emptiness of the Archipelago.

Kanna entered the bridge.

"Not a cloud in the sky," Caleb said with a grim voice.

"I'd rather die in the sunshine anyway, Caleb. I'm too damn pretty for cloudy days."

Masu squinted at the horizon and stepped to the rail.

"I see them," Caleb said.

In the distance, a Keyowah boat motored toward them, barely visible in the silvery light. Tasi and an older Malaysian man stood at the bow.

"Your father looks well," Caleb said to Masu.

Masu nodded.

"See to them, Masu."

Masu exited the bridge. Within minutes, two dozen Keyowah tribesmen stood on the Tavington deck, stone-faced and silent, holding their rifles close. On the Keyowah boat, Masu paid his respects to the old man, then leaped the distance back to the Tavington ship.

The two yachts pulled away from each other, and the old man raised his right arm to the sky. Caleb raised his arm in response.

As the Tavington yacht motored on, Masu and Tasi sat at the front of the group of Keyowah tribesmen.

On the bridge, Kanna shook his head. "Jesus, Caleb," he said. "That's a rough-looking bunch."

But Caleb's attention was focused on the near distance. "Company," he said.

Kanna looked out to open sea and spied a ship coming toward them, John Ellis visible on the deck. "God bless you, John," he said. "Hard to keep that bastard away from a good fight."

Both yachts slowed as they approached each other. Twenty yards apart, they killed their engines and floated closer together. Ellis saluted, smiling behind a cigarette. Soon, less than five yards separated the two bows.

"Good to see you, John," Caleb called out.

Ellis spat into the ocean and gave Caleb a wry grin. "Wife gave me hell, Caleb. Said better men than I decided long ago that the Ellises and the Tavingtons would always stand together."

Caleb nodded. "It'll be a hard day," he said.

"I have a feeling," Ellis laughed, "they're all going to be hard from now on."

Caleb smiled. He turned back to the bridge and gave Kanna a thumbs-up.

John Ellis spun on his heel and walked back to his own bridge. His boat swung wide and fell in behind. The flotilla moved forward, leaving the old Malaysian man watching from the Keyowah boat.

• • • •

As the horizon gradually lightened in the face of the coming day, a dozen Zodiacs ran silently onto the beach at Katalo Island.

Caleb and his force moved quickly to the safety of the jungle and used that cover to make their way along the beach. Along the way, they passed six rebel boats moored on the shoreline, deck guns covered by tarps.

Caleb motioned his men into the jungle and they followed a well-worn path inland.

At a high point in the trail, Tasi touched Caleb on the shoulder. Caleb nodded. The Keyowah melted into the jungle like ghosts.

Kanna and John Ellis took separate groups into the jungle on opposite sides of the trail.

Caleb and his remaining men settled into positions twenty yards back from the others. By this point, the sun had begun to crest the far horizon, its rays purpling the sky overheard. In the deep foliage of the Katalo jungle, however, everything was still darkness and shadow.

Caleb pulled Samuel in close. "Aim low," he whispered. "Squeeze your shots off gently, like you're tickling a baby. If you pull, you miss."

Samuel blinked wide eyes, his glance shifting nervously left to right.

"And stay close to me," Caleb continued. "Whatever else you do, stay close to me."

Samuel nodded, licked his lips, and wiped sweat from his face. Even in the coolness before daybreak, the interior jungle was beginning to heat up. Caleb watched Samuel closely, checked the boy's rifle and then his knife.

Kanna appeared suddenly behind them and leaned in. "If you need to use the knife," he said to Samuel, "just slash, don't stab. Hold your pistol in close and slash wide with the knife." He smiled. "Don't worry, boyo. Tavingtons were born for days like this."

Samuel's face was white with fear. "Nobody was born for days like this," he said.

Kanna moved away into the underbrush.

After a few moments, the tense silence was broken by the sound of heavy footsteps coming from deeper in the jungle. A single-file line of rebel soldiers appeared at the far end of the trail.

Samuel gripped his rifle, hands shaking, and jammed the stock against his shoulder.

"Tasi first," Caleb said, "then us."

Samuel nodded.

Ten yards from Tasi's position, however, the rebel column came to a sudden halt. A low whistle sounded and, without any other warning, the line of the rebels disappeared into the jungle on both sides of the trail.

Caleb whistled, sharp and shrill. An answering whistle came from Tasi's position. Kanna appeared out of the jungle beside Samuel. He flashed a quick hand signal to Caleb.

"Stay close to me, Sam," Caleb said. "This is bad."

The air suddenly came alive. Sizzling specialty rounds exploded through the surrounding jungle, blowing through trees and men alike. Caleb forced Samuel down to the ground, pushing him hard against the trunk of a giant rubber tree. The barrage of heavy fire continued, with Caleb unable to return fire, crouched low. Not all of his men had managed to find shelter, many caught out of position by the unexpected rebel action. In just a few seconds of damage, the Tavington force took heavy casualties.

After the initial barrage, the rebel fire lulled, then stopped altogether. All around Caleb, the screams of injured Tavington men filled the air.

Caleb scrambled to his feet, rifle high. "Up," he shouted to his men. "Eyes up."

He reached down and pulled Samuel to a ready position by his collar. As he did so, dozens of rebel soldiers attacked out of the jungle all around them. The numbers were overwhelming, and they swarmed in as the Tavington men reeled from the storm of bullets that had taken them so completely by surprise. The rebels came with small arms blazing, along with machetes and short blades.

At the same time, rebel snipers hidden high above them in the tress began raining down bullets on Caleb and his men.

It was chaos and death from every direction, including up.

Caleb spun, firing, firing, firing, every shot taking down a rebel soldier. He was like a machine, calmly killing everything that moved.

He pulled Samuel close. "Back to the beach," he yelled. "Go."

Tasi's Keyowah dropped back to Caleb's position, men dying all around. The Keyowah fought like wild animals, slashing serrated machetes at the up-close rebels and emptying magazines of ammunition.

The rebel soldiers flowed in from every side, throwing themselves at the Tavington men in waves. It was frenzied, brutal and bloody.

Caleb and his men retreated through the jungle toward the beach, taking heavy losses. The air pulsated with the sound of bullets whining and men screaming.

Tasi gathered his men around Caleb. He pointed to six of them, and the six immediately handed their necklaces to Tasi.

"Fight well," Caleb said, his breath heaving.

John Ellis and his men finally caught up to Caleb's group, and they were a mess, covered in blood and gore. Caleb motioned them to the beach, and they sprinted by.

Samuel eyed the six Keyowah who had given up their necklaces. "What's going on?" he asked Caleb.

"They're staying," Caleb answered.

The six Keyowah formed a loose line to face the oncoming rebel force. Tasi and Caleb spun and led their remaining men back toward the Zodiacs. In a stumbling run, weapons high, the Tavington force burst out of the jungle onto the beach.

At the shoreline, the tarps covering the six rebel boats flew off, revealing rebel soldiers manning the .50-cal deck guns. The guns opened fire on the Tavington force, obliterating the first of Caleb's men to reach the sand.

Tasi's Keyowah reacted instantly. They ignored the bullets and the chaos around them and began a steady, sniping fire at the rebels on the .50s. Caleb dropped to one knee, pulling Samuel down with him.

"Get behind me, Sam," he shouted.

Samuel pushed Caleb's arm off him, his face strangely calm. "I'm alright, Caleb," he answered, and there was no hint of strain or fear in his voice.

Together, Caleb and Samuel fired on the rebel boats. The Keyowah maintained their kneeling line, completely focused even under the heavy barrage from the rebels. Their steady accuracy eventually cleared the .50-cal guns, but the cost was high.

Caleb scanned his surroundings. Bodies littered the beach. The damage was immense, a cataclysm of death. The Tavington men who were left ran toward the Zodiacs, dragging and carrying their wounded.

From beyond the breakers, the Tavington and Ellis yachts sped toward the beach. Already, the deck guns were firing. The survivors changed their running line, dismissing the Zodiacs and angling toward the incoming boats.

The yachts roared in, sliding to a hard idle just clear of the shallows. As the Tavington force reached the boats, dozens more rebel soldiers streamed out of the jungle, sending a hail of bullets toward the yachts. The Tavington men dragged themselves on board as the Keyowah provided cover fire.

Finally, all of the men were out of the water and the boats pulled away from the shoreline. The Keyowah continued to empty clip after clip into the rebels.

Kanna stood fully upright at the stern of Caleb's boat, screaming defiantly at the rebels, pistols in both hands, soaked in blood.

Caleb grabbed Samuel. "Come with me," he shouted.

He dragged Samuel below deck and into a small room stocked with explosives: touch-sensitive limpet mines, modified claymores, and rocket-propelled grenades. He gave Samuel a handheld rocket launcher and a bag of RPGs, then grabbed a launcher himself. Together, they scrambled back up the stairs.

On deck, Caleb loaded his launcher and sent an RPG straight into the center of the rebel group on the beach, then speed-loaded another explosive round and fired again. Samuel, strangely composed in the chaos and death, followed Caleb's example, firing, loading and firing again in the space of mere seconds. The rebels scrambled for cover, deserting the beach for the safety of the jungle.

Caleb turned Samuel's shoulder and pointed at the rebel boats still anchored along the shoreline.

The Tavington yacht swung wide on its exit line, then came back around for a second, slow pass. Caleb and Samuel locked in their sights and fired every RPG in the bag at the rebel ships, blasting them apart, crippling them where they sat. Leaving a trail of smoke and destruction in their wake, the Tavington boats motored out to open sea.

As the engines settled into high gear, Caleb surveyed the ship's main deck, slippery with blood and guts, bodies strewn everywhere. Wounded men thrashed wildly, screaming and crying, gurgling blood. The uninjured worked desperately to staunch blood flow from dozens of gushing wounds. Tourniquets were applied to tattered limbs, with morphine and adrenaline being pumped liberally into broken bodies.

The eerie sound of a rosary being shouted blended with the screams of the dying. Masu, bleeding from half a dozen wounds, caught Caleb's eye and shook his head. On the Ellis ship, it was an identical scene: the dead and the dying, the attempts to save the wounded, the immense carnage.

Samuel wiped sweat and blood from his eyes. "Today was the day, Caleb," he said as he stared around him. "The day that you were wrong and it got them all killed."

Caleb nodded. "And tomorrow might be the same...and the next day," he responded. "Now, check your weapon, Sam. Always check your weapon. You never know how soon you might need it again."

Samuel pulled the pistol out of his waistband and checked it. He turned to face an approaching Kanna, a strange new look on his face. "No one was born for days like this," he said, voice thick with emotion, then hurried away to help with the wounded.

Kanna watched him go. "They were waitin', Caleb," he said.

"I know."

"Damn it all," Kanna added with venom.

"I know."

· · · ·

Later, Caleb stood in the bow of his yacht, a statue, frozen in place by circumstance. The bodies of the dead had been wrapped in sheets, now blood-soaked, and were lined up in rows on the deck. The priest's voice drifted over the horrific scene, the cadence of his words adding an even greater weight to the moment.

The wounded sat like zombies, propped up against any support, pumped full of morphine.

Samuel moved from man to man, speaking softly with each, smiling, encouraging. He moved with the weariness of battle, but there was a determination on his face, a strength that had not been there the night before.

Caleb's attention was drawn to smoke on the horizon, and he focused in on the source. Within a few moments, Tasi's father's boat came into clear view, completely engulfed in flames. Caleb's yacht slowed as it approached the burning Keyowah boat.

The scene that greeted the Tavington and Keyowah men was a grisly one. Tasi's father's body hung from the bow. It swung slowly in the sea breeze, only feet from the deep blue ocean below.

The Tavington yacht pulled alongside. Masu, Tasi, and the other Keyowah warriors leaped from the bow of Caleb's yacht onto the burning boat. Tasi pulled his father gently up onto the deck, paying no mind at all to the flames and billowing smoke. Masu disappeared down into the hold and returned with a multicolored Keyowah cloth. As the tattered remnant of Tavington men watched in silence, the two brothers wrapped the old man's body in the cloth and laid it flat on the deck. The five Keyowah warriors joined Tasi and Masu, forming a circle around their father. With every head bowed, Tasi said a few words, to which the men responded in unison, then again, and a third time. After the third response, the warriors turned as one and, without a backward glance, leaped the distance back to the Tavington boat, leaving the old man on the burning ship.

Caleb walked forward to Masu and Tasi. "I'm sorry," he simply said, his voice thick.

Tasi turned, and there was no emotion on his face as he replied. "We have not seen days like this before, my brother. Not like this."

"No," Caleb agreed. "No, we have not. But you and I are still standing, brother."

Tasi nodded. "The mother chooses," he said. "It is not up to us."

Caleb took one last long look at the burning Keyowah boat. "I will miss him. He was like a father to me."

"There will be time to grieve," Tasi answered, "yours and mine..."

"After," Caleb said.

"After," Tasi repeated.

Across the water, the Ellis boat veered away, John Ellis at the stern, blood-soaked bandage swathed around his head. He held his right arm up in a salute, which Caleb returned.

Kanna walked up beside Caleb. "Caleb, some of these," he said, indicating the crew, "are hangin' by a thread. You're the only god they ever knew. You should probably be sittin' with 'em when they head off to meet the real one."

Caleb nodded, his lips set in a grim line. He walked back with Kanna and began to circulate among the wounded.

. . . .

The Tavington yacht slowed its engine as it motored alongside the reef of a large coral island. Standing at the bow with Tasi, Caleb turned and motioned Samuel forward.

"Pay attention, Sam," he said. "This reef is tricky, and the Keyowah have made it trickier. None of this is in the map book."

The yacht cut its speed even more. Caleb pointed to a marker on the shore.

"That marker indicates a false cut in the reef. The cut only runs for about fifty yards, then it ends." He pointed toward an interior landmark. "That ridge marks the true cut." As soon as he said the words, the yacht turned into a narrow chasm in the reef. "And it veers sharply at that marker."

Moments later, the yacht cut left and continued on through the reef. Samuel looked up. Dozens of steel wire rope cables ran from a cliff on one side of the bay to a high point on the other side of the bay. The cables hung only ten feet above the deck of the Tavington yacht.

"What are those?" he asked.

Caleb gave Samuel a tight smile. "That's part of the Keyowah welcome for uninvited guests."

Up ahead, many Keyowah lined the beach, waiting for the yacht to pull into shore. Caleb turned to Tasi.

"You and I have much to do, brother," he said.

Tasi nodded, eyes hard. "We seek only the will of the mother, Caleb...and a chance to die with honor. There is a traitor in your tribe, and today he killed twenty Keyowah warriors without firing a single shot."

Caleb held Tasi's eyes, and there was a world of vengeance in their look. "You and I have much to do," he said again.

• • • •

Later, as the fading afternoon sun turned toward evening, the Tavington yacht made its final approach to the reef outside Seti Bay. The number of wrapped bodies on deck had grown, and it was obvious that many of the remaining men would not survive the day. Heatwaves danced along the deck, drifting up from the stains of blood, vomit and gore.

Once through the gap in the reef, the yacht anchored just off the beach in the shallows. On the sand, a crowd of women and children had gathered. Caleb and the few remaining able-bodied men jumped into the waist-deep water and began the grim task of offloading the dead and wounded.

As the bodies of the dead were brought into the beach and identified, the cries of the families filled the air, heart-wrenching screams of pain and loss. Body after body was laid on the sand, each one wrapped in a blood-crusted cloth that had hardened in the sun.

When the deck was finally empty and the last body had been reunited with its waiting family, Caleb stood frozen in the water, watching the scene on shore with an empty look on his face.

Emma appeared at the edge of the crowd and stopped, her eyes wide with fear as she scanned the bodies. Finally, she spotted him in the water and relief flooded her face.

Caleb returned her stare, numb, showing no reaction at all. Emma waded out into the water and, without words, she took him into her arms.

The cries of anguish on the beach increased, the otherworldly sounds of loss and ache.

"Today was the day, Em," Caleb said in a voice totally flat and devoid of life. "The day I was wrong and it killed all of them. Today was the day."

He stared down at the water. Unable to continue talking, he simply shut his eyes and covered them with both hands, then sank down until he was completely submerged. Emma supported his weight as he hung, suspended and lifeless. Finally, she pulled him gently back above the surface.

"Caleb," she began, her voice soft but firm, "you're only human. You do what you can. You've always done what you can. It's why they trust you. It's why they still trust you. It's why I love you."

She cradled his head against her, holding him close. They remained like that for what seemed an eternity, as Caleb struggled against the weight on his shoulders, against the darkness pushing down on him, smothering him.

Long minutes passed, and his breathing finally settled into a regular rhythm. His body relaxed, and he pushed himself gently away from Emma.

"What are you doing here?" he asked.

. . . .

In the light of the evening moon, the Tavington group sat at a table under a white canopy tent, on the cliffs of Seti Bay. Emma occupied a seat beside Caleb.

White-coated servants hovered, pouring tea and serving light food.

The group was visibly exhausted, bloodshot eyes set deep in weary faces.

On the shore below, Tavington men, many bandaged and limping, loaded the remaining yachts, with women and children helping wherever they could. Samuel walked the shore, talking and laughing, lifting the spirits of the beaten-down Tavington force as he lent a hand with the loading.

From their high vantage point, the group under the tent watched Samuel and the activity below.

"You may be right about Sammy, Caleb," Kanna said. "He's a Tavington...and they love him."

Passo nodded and added, "In the moonlight, he looks just like the old man."

"He is his father's son," Caleb agreed.

Emma reached over and put her hand on Caleb's arm. "And a lot like you were, before the war."

"Aye," Kanna said. "The blood runs hot, and it runs strong."

Caleb looked across the table at Passo. "Would you sail with him, Passo? If he wasn't my brother?"

Passo considered this for a moment, then nodded. "I would," he said. "After today...I would."

Caleb watched Passo for a moment, then turned away, satisfied.

On the beach, a man holding a radio brought it to Samuel. Samuel sprinted up the hill to the command tent. "It's Luke," he announced to the table, breathless.

Caleb took the transmitter, the unit loud with static. "Luke, where the hell are you?" he said into the receiver.

Luke's voice, when it came, was fuzzy and indistinct. "Caleb, can you hear me?" Luke said. "I got hit, Caleb...I got hit. I'm ten miles east of Freetown. The boat is shit...took me a whole day just to wire this radio. I was on my way back and ran right the hell smack into a boat full o' mutts."

Static pushed in again.

"How bad off are you?" Caleb asked.

"I took a bullet in the leg, Caleb...nothing serious. I just can't move this piece of shit. I'm dead water right now. It's gonna be a couple of hours before I can jerry-rig this tin can and get going. What about Katalo? Did you hit them?"

"Katalo was hard, Luke, Katalo was a mess...and we're thin."

Caleb looked at Emma. "Listen carefully, Luke," he continued, raising his voice to be heard above the static. "Tomorrow, we're at Bellamy's Rock."

A long moment of silence followed. Finally, Luke responded. "That's a good choice, Caleb," he said. "Hard to hit. I'll get there, eventually."

"No, Luke," Caleb responded. "I need you to do something else. I need you to go to Council. You're close to Freetown. Council must get a message to Wallace...tell him that we're finished. The Tavingtons request terms of surrender."

Even over the radio, Luke's voice betrayed his surprise. "What?" he asked. "Caleb...did you say 'surrender'? What about Bellamy's Rock? It's a good position to defend."

"We're too far gone, Luke, thinner than Wallace blood. We got hit hard at Katalo and we're taking water. Go to John Ellis. He can help you get to the others. Whatever it takes. We won't survive another attack."

"Are you sure, Caleb? I'll do it, boy, but are you sure?"

"We have no choice. We ask only free passage to Malaysia...safe passage. It's our only condition. If it is accepted, we will go peacefully." Caleb took a deep breath. "Can you do it, Luke?"

"Jesus, boy," Luke replied. "Yeah, I can do that."

"Good," Caleb said. "We're counting on you. Take care of yourself, Luke."

The static on the radio died as the transmission ended. Caleb clicked his receiver off and sat back in his chair. The eyes of all the men now focused on Emma.

"Are you sure, Em?" Kanna asked.

Emma nodded, and her face was drawn. "I'm sure. He stopped and talked to me, Kanna. I'm sorry."

Kanna looked at Caleb. "Maybe he really was trying to smooth things with Black," he said, with the look of a man grasping at straws. "Maybe he decided to take the initiative himself. Maybe?"

Caleb stared at the radio, eyes glazed with anger.

Passo rubbed his eyes, agitated.

"Son of a bitch," Kanna said.

He looked back and forth between Caleb and Passo, then finally exhaled loudly, shaking his head.

"Son of a bitch," he repeated.

• • • •

Miles away, on the bridge of the Wallace family yacht, Luke stared down at the radio in his hand. On the map table in front of him sat a full tumbler of whiskey. Across the table were Black Wallace and Michael. Michael looked terrible, eyes puffy, hair disheveled. He leaned toward his father.

"Father...if they surrender...," Michael began, his voice almost pleading.

"Shut up, boy," Black said.

"But if they surrender"—he glanced at Luke—"we must allow them to surrender. Passage to Malaysia, Father...it's a small thing."

"Michael," Black growled impatiently, "I am an Englishman. If an Englishman applies for surrender, honor offers no course but to accept that surrender. I will allow him what he and his mutt army did not allow the Pawan tribe. Now. Shut. Up."

Michael stared at his father, then at Luke, a glimmer of hope on his face. "It's the right thing, Father," he said, nodding his head vigorously, "the right thing."

Black gave a dismissive nod.

Michael stood and walked shakily to the door. "The right thing," he mumbled as he exited the room.

Luke sighed. He set the radio down on the table. "Caleb Tavington is hard to kill," he said.

Black leaned back in his chair. "Next time," he said, "you and I...we need to be there, Luke. A room full of mutts can't do the job of one good white man, and it's time we stopped hoping for a miracle."

"I think you're right," Luke responded. "But do you really want to stare across the water at him?"

Black's eyes hardened. "There is nothing in heaven or earth," he said, "that I want more."

He leaned forward, all menace and hate.

"Nothing."

· · · ·

At Seti Bay, the group at the table had lapsed into a tired silence, each person lost in their thoughts. Finally, Samuel turned to Caleb.

"Where are we going to go, Caleb?"

Caleb looked out at the horizon. "There are seven hundred and seven islands in this archipelago, Sam," he said, "and they are all too hard to defend when you're as thin as we are...except one. Bellamy's Rock."

Kanna nodded. "And maybe not even one," he added.

"Maybe not." Caleb gave a grim smile. "We'll find out."

"Would they let us surrender," Samuel asked, "and just go?"

"Nobody wants to take any more losses," Caleb answered. "Malaysia is close. If they allowed free passage, we could be out of the Archipelago in a day."

"I wouldn't," Samuel said. "I wouldn't let us go."

Emma smiled sadly at Caleb, exhausted. He grabbed her by the elbow and lifted her out of her chair.

He turned back to the table. "Talk it over," he said, "and be ready at midnight." So saying, he led Emma out of the tent.

• • • •

Minutes later, Caleb and Emma stood in the entryway of their tent, watching the bay. Large bonfires lit up the night as men and women piled supplies onto the flames. No more loading was taking place, only burning. Samuel walked from fire to fire, silhouetted against the flickering light.

Emma took Caleb's hand and began walking down the slope.

"Where are we going?" Caleb asked.

"Down there," Emma said. "They need you now, Caleb. More than ever. They're frightened and they don't know what tomorrow will bring. They need you beside them."

"Sam's down there, Em."

"And maybe some other night," she replied, "that would be enough, but it's not enough tonight. Tonight, you must be your father to these people. That was part of his strength, Caleb. He could lead when he didn't have a gun in his hand."

Emma stopped and looked up into Caleb's face. "And so can you."

Emma walked hand in hand with Caleb down the slope to the fires. They circulated among the people, Caleb taking his cue from a radiant, smiling Emma. She moved from one group to the next, helping with anything she could, striking up conversations, laughing or consoling where needed. The Tavington men, women and children clearly responded to her energy and graciousness.

Caleb smiled, watching Emma. He said a few encouraging words to as many people as he could, and they crowded around, heartened by his presence.

Caleb and Emma stayed on the beach until all of the people had gone. Only Samuel remained with them. He smiled, dead on his feet, saluted Emma and Caleb, then made his way slowly up the slope to his tent.

Alone on the beach, Caleb and Emma stood for a time, staring out at the stars and the black Archipelago ocean below.

"So beautiful," she whispered. "And so dangerous." She continued on, voice strained. "She gives and she takes, blessed be the sea that binds us."

Caleb put his arm around her. "This is all I've ever known," he said thoughtfully. "The Archipelago. I've never aspired to anything else. Until you."

Emma looked up into Caleb's eyes, then pulled his face down into a kiss. "The sea that binds us," she said again.

They stood together for a while longer, watching the fires die down, feeling the cold creep in from the midnight expanse in front of them.

Finally, Emma pushed herself away, and the pain of it was clear on her face. Tears welled up in her eyes, but she walked slowly up the hillside without a backward glance.

Caleb scanned the ridgeline, noticed the shadows of his men moving about in the moonlight. He pushed a log back from a nearby fire and sat down to wait.

CHAPTER THIRTEEN

The Archipelago sun sent its first light across Bellamy's Rock, a coral atoll overgrown with jungle, protected from the ocean by high cliff walls along the coastline. At first glance, the island seemed impregnable, its one point of access a small bay cut into the towering rock all around.

Two Tavington yachts sat in the protected bay. Against the backdrop of massive solid walls, the ships seemed small and fragile.

All around Bellamy's Rock lay smaller islands, a veritable maze of coral protrusions, like a child's dot-to-dot coloring page. Some of these were no larger than a football field. All were covered with vegetation.

The island's greatest protection, however, as was the case with most of the major islands in the Archipelago, was the razor-sharp reef that surrounded it.

Outside of that reef sat a small fleet of enemy rebel yachts, two lines of ten each, facing each other, creating a gauntlet at the end of which waited a third line of ten yachts, the Wallace battle boats. The Wallace boats faced the opening of Bellamy's Rock Bay.

On the Wallace deck ramparts, their .50-cal guns were protected behind steel enclosures, shielding the gunners. Unlike the Tavington yachts, the Wallace gun enclosures were sealed without a gap. The gunners were completely protected once the entry hatch was closed.

Luke stood in the bridge of the last boat in the western rebel line, the boat furthest from the bay and closest to the Wallace yachts.

Directly opposite Luke on the eastern line of rebel yachts, Captain Wahroo stood on the bow of his own boat, facing the bay.

• • • •

On the Tavington bridge, Caleb stared out into the new dawn, with Kanna and Masu just behind him. Masu lit a cigarette off the one he was already smoking.

"Mornings are hard, gentlemen," Caleb said, his voice flat. "If your resolve survives the gauntlet of morning, you just might live forever."

Kanna scanned the waiting lines of enemy boats. "Speaking of bloody gauntlets...," he muttered.

Samuel entered, freshly shaved and alert, no sign of fear on his face. He slipped the pistol from his waistband, checked the clip and tucked it back in. "Lovely day," he said in greeting. "Those cans around the fifties are cute."

Kanna scanned the gun enclosures on the far-off Wallace boats. "Not very friendly," he said. "That's for sure."

Caleb picked up a radio sitting on the map table. He pressed the transmitter, staring at Samuel, Masu, and Kanna. "It's time," he said into the radio.

All four men directed their attention toward the ocean ahead of them.

In front of Caleb's yacht, a power trawler piloted by Passo moved out toward the enemy boats. Passo held a white flag high in the air. It was a surreal sight, the lone boat moving from its sheltered space into danger—the waiting jaws of a lion.

Then, as Passo passed through the cut in the reef, Caleb put his yacht into gear.

Passo's small but solid boat headed directly toward the line of Wallace boats facing the bay, between the lines of rebel yachts.

Caleb's yacht started through the reef, with the second Tavington boat directly behind. Both boats maintained the middle line that Passo had already charted.

- - - -

On the Wallace yacht, Black Wallace was focused on Passo's boat, which continued its steady, slow pace toward him, white flag waving. Michael stood nearby, face like a cadaver. Black picked up a radio.

"Are you ready, my dear Captain?" Black asked into the radio.

Wahroo's voice came back amidst the static. "We are ready," he said.

Black smiled. "Good," he said. "When Tavington is halfway through your position, open fire."

Michael snapped his head around. "What?" he sputtered. "Father, what are you talking about? What—"

"Shut your mouth, boy," Black growled. "Did you really think I was going to let him just walk away?" He snorted in derision. "So he could come back and cut my throat in the night? Safe passage...I'll give him safe passage to the bottom of the ocean."

For Michael, this latest development was too much to bear. He began to break down. His eyes reflected the unraveling that was taking place inside him. "You lied to me," he said.

He stepped forward and grabbed his father by the shirt.

"You lied to me," he repeated, his voice louder this time.

Black backhanded Michael across the face, a powerful blow that knocked Michael back and down to one knee. Head hanging, hair in his face, he began to cry.

"You lied to me," he sobbed.

Black Wallace stared down at his son with contempt. "You're pathetic," he said.

Black turned back to the window, refocusing on Passo and the approaching white-flag boat of surrender.

Down on the floor, Michael lifted his head and stared at his father. An angry red welt had begun to swell under his eye. He pushed himself to his feet and stood in place for a moment, tears flowing down his face, a man teetering on the edge of a cliff. He looked past Black's shoulder at the armada of ships arrayed across the entrance to Bellamy's Rock. For a moment, it looked as if he might say something, but the moment passed and Michael dropped his head. Without a sound, he shuffled out of the bridge and closed the door behind him.

• • • •

On the Tavington yacht, Caleb, Samuel, Kanna and Masu surveyed the line of rebel boats on either side of them as they motored slowly past. Wide smile on his hobgoblin face, Kanna waved at the soldiers, even giving an occasional thumbs-up.

"Like a bloody parade," he gushed. "We've never been so popular. All it took was the end of the world."

The others couldn't help but smile at Kanna's macabre enthusiasm. He was like a kid in a candy store.

Still, their full attention was on Passo and the small boat leading them forward.

• • • •

From his own bridge, Luke watched Passo motor by, his eyes on the fluttering white surrender flag. Passo had now cleared the entire line of rebel boats and was motoring into the empty ocean between the rebels behind him and the Wallace ships facing him.

Luke turned to monitor Caleb's yacht.

"Almost there," he whispered to himself. "Almost. Keep coming, boy. Jesus is waiting."

Movement on the Bellamy's Rock cliff front caught his eye. A dozen Keyowah warriors stepped out of the vegetation and onto the edge of the cliff. Luke lifted a pair of binoculars to his eyes. The Keyowah spread out in a firing line, dropped to one knee and jammed their rifle stocks hard against their shoulders.

"Mother of mercy," Luke said, panic in his voice. He quickly checked the Tavington boats in front of him. Caleb's yacht was close enough now that Luke could see into the Tavington bridge. Caleb, Masu, Kanna and Passo were all staring directly at him.

Then, as Luke watched in horror, a steel wire rope cable hooked to the end of Passo's trawler snapped taut. The far end of the cable was hooked onto a metal rod at the mouth of Bellamy's Rock Bay. The cable pulled tight, lifting out of the water and revealing explosive limpet touch mines all along its hundred-yard length. Canisters of gasoline were attached to the cable on either side of every touch mine.

"Holy shit," Luke breathed and jammed his ship into reverse.

As Luke's engines roared to life, Passo's boat cut hard right, keeping the cable taut and dragging dozens of the improvised gasoline bombs directly into the western line of rebel boats.

At the same time, Caleb's ship swerved from its course, following Passo's lead.

The rebel ships were frozen in their positions, completely unprepared for the attack from the Tavingtons. Only Luke reacted, his engines digging hard as he reversed away from the touch mines skimming across the surface of the water toward him. No other rebel ship even moved.

Passo pulled the cable lined with touch mines and gasoline into the rebels, and the entire western line of boats erupted into chaos. The mines made contact with the rebel hulls, setting off their explosive charges and detonating the gasoline canisters like firebombs. The air was filled with smoke and flame and the sound of explosions.

As it swerved backwards away from the rebel line, Luke's boat narrowly missed a touch mine, and somehow the boat next to him also avoided the mines. All of the rest of the rebel boats in the western line were on fire.

Luke spun the wheel, eyes frantically checking his clearance from the boats all around him. The scene was absolute confusion. He worked the engine, jumping forward, then reversing again, in an attempt to reach open ocean.

As Luke and the boat beside him cleared the touch mines, the two Tavington yachts came roaring out of the smoke and chaos and were immediately on top of them. The Tavington .50-cal guns opened fire on Luke's boat. Before Luke could gather himself and take any further evasive action, the Tavington boats slammed alongside. Tavington men swarmed onto his deck, leaping the distance over the water as the hulls ground against each other.

The Tavington pirates were like men possessed. They threw themselves at their enemy, overwhelming Luke's men with sheer frenzied brutality. Short blades and machetes flashed in the morning sunlight, hacking and stabbing without quarter. The air was filled with screams and the rapid-fire pop-pop-pop of close-quarter weapons. In addition, the heavier rattling of the .50s created a wall of solid sound. Luke's bridge disintegrated around him under the Tavington turreted guns. He scrambled along the floor, covering his face from the shattering glass and splintering wood, then stumbled down the stairs and out onto the deck.

In the madness of the battle on deck, Caleb stood waiting for his cousin, his face like ice. Luke fumbled for the pistol in his waistband, but it was too late. Caleb exploded into Luke, knocking the pistol into the ocean.

As the fighting raged all around them, Caleb and Luke squared off, each with a long knife in hand. Caleb smiled, a cold, menacing smile, and in it there was only death. It was the smile of someone who knew without the shadow of a doubt that he had been born for moments like this. Luke licked his suddenly dry lips. The prospect of facing Caleb Tavington was not one that even the most hardened man would relish. He shifted his balance nervously, breath coming in short gasps now.

Caleb wasted no time, attacking Luke like a whirlwind, his blade flashing in a blur. Within seconds, Luke had sustained deep wounds all over his torso.

Luke took a few steps backward, a desperate fear in his eyes. He hadn't even been close to getting a blade onto Caleb in the flurry.

"Caleb," he sputtered, voice breaking, "stop...I—"

Caleb didn't give Luke the chance to finish. There was a wildness in his eyes, a reflection of something primal and dangerous inside him. He lunged in, parried Luke's thrust with a casual fend, and buried his blade deep in Luke's throat.

"Save your breath," Caleb growled, "for dying."

Luke gurgled out an unintelligible sentence. His eyes locked onto Caleb's. His hands pulled at Caleb's face, as if he wanted to draw him closer and tell him something.

"I don't care what you're trying to say, Luke," Caleb said. "I don't care why you did it. I don't want to hear your reasons. I'm only here for one thing." So saying, he pushed the knife into Luke's throat, all the way to the hilt.

• • • •

On the Wallace yacht, Black Wallace stared at the scene playing out in front of him. The entire western line of rebel boats was in complete disarray. Most of the ships were on fire and taking water.

He picked up the radio. "Blow those boats out of the water," he ordered.

The remaining line of rebel boats began to move forward, toward the decimated western line. The rebel soldiers swiveled the .50-cal guns from side to side, sweeping the chaos in front of them, attempting to lock in on the Tavington boats. The billowing smoke and fire, however, made it almost impossible for the guns to find a clear target.

• • • •

Meanwhile, the battle on Luke's boat was over. The devastating Tavington attack had completely overwhelmed Luke's crew. Caleb's men had taken over both Luke's boat and the one beside it, the only other rebel boat in the western line that had survived the bomb attack.

Caleb walked the length of the bloodied deck and stood staring through the smoke at Black Wallace's boat. In his right hand, he held Luke's decapitated head. He thrust it high into the air for Black Wallace and everyone else to see, then hurled it into the ocean and spat in Black's direction.

As the remaining line of rebel yachts closed the distance to Caleb and his men, the Keyowah on the cliff opened fire, a hail of deadly-accurate specialty rounds. The rapid-fire sizzling of the bullets could be heard even above the sounds of the wounded and the roaring of the onboard fires. The expert Keyowah marksmen quickly cleared the big guns, raining a blanket of death down on the rebel boats. Wahroo's men were thrown into panicked confusion, sheltering behind any cover they could find. In the face of the consistent deadly fire, they could do nothing but hide.

As the rebels wilted under the heavy Keyowah barrage, the four boats now under Caleb's control lurched full throttle toward the advancing rebel line, avoiding ships on fire as they threaded their way through heavy smoke. Caleb's .50s opened fire, adding to the chaos on the rebel ships.

On deck, Masu handed a radio to Caleb. Caleb focused on one of the outlying coral islands behind the approaching line of rebel boats. The island, one of the maze of small vegetation-covered coral atolls around Bellamy's Rock, sat roughly halfway between the bay and the line of Wallace boats facing the bay.

Caleb lifted the radio. "Whenever you're ready, John," he said into the receiver.

Along the front of the small island, a netting of camouflage dropped to the ocean's surface, revealing a hollow outcropping behind it, an open-sided cave cut naturally into the coral walls. Waiting under the outcropping were two yachts, outfitted for a fight, tripod-mounted .50-cals lining the rails. John Ellis stood at the bow of one of the ships.

The two Ellis ships roared out into open sea, .50s firing.

The rebel line was a shambles, facing fire from Caleb and his four ships in the front and the Ellis ships in the back.

Caleb's ships closed the distance to the reeling rebel line at speed.

• • • •

On the rapidly disintegrating bridge of the lead rebel boat, Captain Wahroo cowered behind an overturned map table, blood spurting from a gash across his forehead. He managed a glance out of his shattered front window.

The sight that greeted him forced a sudden, tremulous intake of breath. Barreling directly toward him was Caleb Tavington's yacht, .50-cal guns blazing.

• • • •

On the Tavington deck, Caleb knelt by the bow rail, firing an automatic rifle with deadly accuracy, taking out rebel soldiers on Captain Wahroo's ship as his yacht ate up the distance. Samuel scrambled up beside him, settled into a kneeling position and lifted his own rifle. Caleb looked over.

"Stay close to me," he shouted over the roaring of the engines and the gunfire.

Samuel answered without taking his focus off the rebel boats ahead. "What?"

Caleb looked at Samuel as if seeing him for the first time. Samuel grinned, confident and unafraid.

Caleb smiled in response. "Never mind," he said.

All four of the Tavington boats charged in toward Wahroo's ships, full throttle, the distance now less than ten yards. Caleb and Samuel braced themselves for impact. All around them, Tavington men crowded the deck.

At the last moment, Caleb's yacht swung its bow and slammed into the side of Wahroo's yacht with a crash of splintering wood and metal.

The Tavington men, led by Caleb and Samuel, swarmed the rebel yacht with ferocious screams, emptying their weapons and slashing with knives and machetes. They were madmen, wild as the Archipelago that had bred them, taking their cue from a hacking, slashing, relentless Caleb. Masu shadowed Caleb in the fighting, his wicked-looking Keyowah blade flashing like a propeller in the sunlight.

Just across the water, Ellis and his two boats were engaged in furious hand-to-hand combat with the crew of two rebel boats they had successfully boarded.

Even as the close-quarter fighting intensified, the Keyowah continued to snipe the rebel line with unerring accuracy, bringing down rebel soldiers even in the crowded confusion of the battle.

The fighting on board Wahroo's yacht was intense, but the Tavington men were simply not to be denied their victory. Like animals caught in a trap, they ripped and tore their way through the rebel soldiers opposing them.

In only a few terrible minutes, the fighting was over.

Caleb, shirtless and bloodstained, stood on the deck with Samuel and Masu. Samuel looked a mess, covered in blood, a large gash over one eye. As he scanned the deck for signs of continued resistance, he tore off a portion of his shirt and wrapped it around his head. Once it was clear that the rebels had no fight left, the men turned and stared out at the Wallace boats, which had maintained their line, unmoving, throughout the battle.

"What's he waiting for?" Samuel asked, wiping blood and sweat out of his eyes.

Caleb shook his head.

On the boats all around them, the same scene was playing out—rebel soldiers laying down their weapons and surrendering. It was a surreal vista: boats on fire, many obviously taking water, decks littered with the dead and the dying, bodies floating in the open ocean and the air filled with acrid black smoke. The water around Bellamy's Rock was a scene of pure carnage.

A commotion began at the bridge end of the ship. Caleb's men dragged Wahroo out of the stairwell and pushed him roughly across the deck to stand in front of Caleb. Caleb stepped toward the captain. A silence descended on the deck. Even the cries of the wounded seemed muted as Caleb spoke.

"You have no honor," he said, with complete disdain for the man standing in front of him. "No code. He saw this, Black Wallace. He saw that you have the soul of a pig. Your inadequacy killed my father. For that, you must die."

Wahroo lifted his head. "Kill me," he responded with as much bravery as he could muster. "You will not survive to enjoy your small victory."

"Englishmen do not kill their prisoners," he said and turned his back on Wahroo. He nodded to Masu. "Masu."

Masu stepped forward, Keyowah blade in hand. He motioned to Kanna, who slid a machete along the deck. The blade stopped at Wahroo's feet. Wahroo bent down and picked it up.

In the near distance, the Wallace battle boats began to motor slowly forward.

"Make it quick, Masu," Caleb said. "He's coming."

Masu slid forward, face set in stone. He looked for all the world like an executioner preparing for his work.

Wahroo stared around at the crowd of men gathering. His own soldiers had been herded against a deck railing under the shadow of the bridge. Most of them had their heads down or were staring at the ocean below.

The Tavington men formed a large circle, giving the two combatants plenty of room for what was to come.

Wahroo hefted his blade, then charged. Masu deflected Wahroo's thrust, stepped in casually and head-butted Wahroo, who crumpled to the deck. As Wahroo fell, Masu's blade lashed out. The captain screamed, grabbing the side of his head, and scrambled away.

Masu reached down and picked Wahroo's ear up off the deck.

The captain got to his feet and charged again. Masu sidestepped, sliding deftly clear, and smacked the back of Wahroo's head with the flat of his blade. As Wahroo turned, Masu's machete flicked out and sliced off Wahroo's remaining ear. Wahroo's head jerked back and, with a snap thrust, Masu took out Wahroo's right eye. Wahroo fell backwards with a scream. In desperation, he threw his blade at Masu's head. Lightning-quick, Masu caught the blade in midflight, flipped it, caught it by the handle, then stepped forward and slashed out Wahroo's other eye.

Wahroo dropped to his knees.

Caleb made a series of hand motions, and the watching Tavington men rushed to their battle stations, preparing to defend the ship against the coming Wallace assault. They herded the rebel prisoners to the end of the deck and pushed them all into the ocean.

Masu grabbed Wahroo by the shirt and hauled him to his feet. "You killed my father," he said, his voice low and coarse. "Your own family is now forfeit. They will never be safe. Think about that as your men let you drown."

So saying, Masu dragged Wahroo, now blind, to the edge of the deck. He slammed him against the deck rail, then upended him over the rail into the ocean. When Wahroo hit the water, none of his men made any effort to help him. Instead, they swam for their lives toward Bellamy's Rock and the other nearby islands.

Wahroo splashed and sputtered frantically for a few moments on the surface of the water, then screamed and went under.

Samuel stepped forward and stood next to Masu. He stared at the spot where Wahroo had been.

"Nice day for a swim," he said.

Around them, a flurry of activity was taking place on deck as the Tavingtons settled into their positions.

Caleb tapped Samuel on the shoulder. "Time to go, gentlemen," he said. "That sound you hear is your life slipping away." He turned to Kanna. "Whatever happens, protect her, Kanna. If it looks lost, run hard. Keep her well."

Kanna nodded. "On my life, Caleb," he promised. "On my life."

One of the Ellis boats slipped alongside the Tavington yacht.

Kanna began shouting orders, and most of the Tavington men leaped the distance to the Ellis yacht. Kanna gripped Caleb's forearm, and the two men nodded at each other, two front-line soldiers saying goodbye. With one last look around, Kanna made the leap to the deck of the Ellis yacht.

John Ellis walked to the rail directly opposite of where Caleb was standing. "Fight well, Caleb boy," he called out.

"Fight well, John," Caleb responded.

The Ellis boat churned the water and sped away, joining the remaining Tavington boats, who swung around wide and motored back toward Bellamy's Rock Bay.

Caleb walked quickly across the deck, making himself clearly visible to the approaching Wallace yachts. Samuel joined him. Once they had established to the Wallace line that both Tavingtons remained on the yacht, he and Samuel scrambled up the stairs to the bridge. Caleb slammed the boat into gear and sped off to open ocean.

. . . .

On the Wallace bridge, Black grabbed the radio, his eyes on Caleb's yacht.

"Tanner," he said, "stay with Tavington. He's breaking to blue water."

Within seconds, four of the Wallace yachts burst forward and out of the line. They swung wide and followed Caleb's yacht toward the horizon.

Black watched for a moment or two, then turned his attention to Bellamy's Rock Bay and the rest of the Tavington force sheltered within it.

"Clay," he said into the radio. "Take yours and blow the Tavingtons out of that rock."

He set the radio down, jammed his yacht into gear and swerved away from Bellamy's Rock, tracking the line of Caleb's ship toward open ocean.

. . . .

On Caleb's yacht, Samuel stared back at Bellamy's Rock, keeping an eye on the Wallace battle boats.

He squinted his eyes against the glare of the Archipelago sun.

"We've got four coming," he said.

Caleb nodded without turning back.

"And now five," Samuel added. "Black is on."

Samuel took a few moments to assess the condition of their yacht—splintered deck, large gaps in the hull, and a bridge that was falling apart.

With a frown, he said, "She's in pretty bad shape, Caleb."

Caleb laughed. "We're in God's hands now, Sam," he answered.

The few Tavington soldiers left on board took their positions against the deck rail along the stern, rifles ready. In spite of its condition, the yacht managed to maintain its speed.

The Wallace yachts, however, gradually closed ground. Once in range, the firefight erupted, with the powerful .50-cal guns hammering away at the Tavington yacht, forcing Caleb into jarring evasive maneuvers.

The Tavington men were excellent marksmen, keeping the Wallace soldiers under cover, but no amount of small-caliber fire could clear the shielded Wallace guns. The big .50-cals rained damage down on Caleb's ship, pulverizing wood and steel and glass.

Caleb's mastery on the water kept his yacht from taking too much heavy fire. He slipped back and forth, forcing the Wallace boats to swerve around each other to avoid collisions. Still, it was obvious that the situation couldn't last long. The Tavington ship was on its last legs.

CHAPTER FOURTEEN

The water outside of Bellamy's Rock Bay was a graveyard of burning and broken ships. Dozens of bodies floated in the debris. The surface of the ocean was slick with oil and blood, shimmering like trails of glitter in the Archipelago sun.

Inside the bay, sheltered by the surrounding reef and cliff walls on either side, the remaining Tavington and Ellis yachts formed a ragged line, facing the Wallace boats outside the reef, under the command of Clay Abelard.

At the base of the cliffs on either side of the bay mouth, Tavington men scrambled over the rocks to a set of concrete bunkers built directly into the cliffside. On top of each bunker, the men pulled back large camouflage tarps, revealing .50-cal guns mounted into the concrete. The guns had unobstructed firing lines through one hundred yards of open water approaching the bay.

On John Ellis's yacht inside the bay, John walked up beside Kanna, casually smoking a cigarette. Even though his shirtsleeve was soaked with blood, he seemed as relaxed as if he was on a pleasure cruise.

He and Kanna stood for a few moments, staring out at the Wallace boats beyond the reef.

"Who are we starin' at?" John asked through a stream of smoke.

"Clay," Kanna answered.

Ellis spat into the ocean. "Looks like he's havin' a little trouble makin' up his little mind," he said.

"Hmmm. Looks like it...a little."

Ellis smiled. His eyes narrowed as he scanned the decks facing them. "We'll have a hell of a time crackin' those .50s if he ever finds his backbone."

. . . .

On the lead Wallace boat, Clay stood at the window of the bridge, staring into Bellamy's Rock Bay. He assessed the .50s pointing directly at him, then swept his eyes up to the line of Keyowah sharpshooters on the cliff. He shuffled his feet like a man waiting for bad news. Finally, he picked up the radio and turned to his wheelman.

"With them fitties in the rocks and the mutts up on the cliff, this one's goin' be a son of a bitch."

The wheelman nodded.

Clay clenched his jaw. He gave the scene in front of him another long look, fidgeting with the radio.

The wheelman cleared his throat. "Only fools...rush in," he offered.

Clay nodded and lifted the radio to his mouth.

. . . .

Back on the Ellis yacht, John Ellis finished his cigarette and flicked it into the ocean. Beside him, Kanna barked out a laugh.

"I'll be damned," he said.

Outside the reef, Clay's boat and the other four turned toward open ocean and motored away.

"Yes," Ellis responded with a smile, "undoubtedly you will...but not today."

. . . .

Miles away, Caleb's yacht was approaching the Keyowah island, Tasi's home.

The damaged Tavington ship was somehow maintaining its separation from the pursuing Wallace boats. Directly behind it, Tanner led the chase, with one other boat close on his wake. The other three Wallace yachts had fallen back slightly, with Black Wallace bringing up the rear.

On the bridge, Samuel kept his eyes rearward.

"We've got two up close, Caleb," he said. "That's Tan. Eamon is way back."

Caleb nodded and cut his speed slightly, allowing Tanner to close the gap. They were hard onto the island now, the water lightening in front of them as they approached the reef. Caleb eyed the shoreline and waited for his marker. He decreased his speed even more, angling along the edge of the coral barrier.

Tanner's ship and the second Wallace ship made up the distance quickly, barreling in so close that Samuel could see Tanner's face through the window of the bridge, across the separating water.

"Tanner's right there, Caleb. Boat length back, now," Samuel advised.

Caleb nodded, still watching the shoreline. Reaching his marker, he glanced back at Tanner's boat, then swerved hard into the gap in the reef. As soon as he saw that Tanner had also made the reef-scraping turn, he locked the wheel into place.

"Let's dance, Sam," he said.

With one last look at the boats behind them, Samuel and Caleb scrambled down the stairs.

· · · ·

On deck, the remaining Tavington men huddled behind cover, shielding themselves from the continuing fire from Tanner's boat.

Caleb and Samuel burst through the stairwell door.

"With me," Caleb shouted over the gunfire.

Caleb got his bearings once again from the shore markers. He glanced quickly up at the steel wire rope cables strung across the mouth of the bay, just above the reef. He lifted his hand above his head, checking to make sure that his men were focused on him.

"Now." He dropped his hand and shouted the order.

Head down, he sprinted across the deck into the wind. Samuel and the rest of the men raced after him. At the bow rail, Caleb leaped high into the air, vaulted off the rail and out over the ocean. He stretched out in midflight and hit the water in a clean dive. Within seconds, Samuel and the remaining men had all done the same, clearing the inner edge of the razor reef by mere feet.

Behind them, the Tavington yacht slammed into the reef at the end of the false cut. The front end of the boat collapsed in a mass of twisted metal and splintered wood.

Without even one second to react, Tanner plowed full throttle into the stern of the Tavington ship. The sound of the impact was like a bomb going off on the water, and the ship slammed to a crushing halt. Caught off-balance, Tanner flew through the window of the bridge to the deck below, his body crumpling in a heap with a loud thud.

Seconds later, the boat behind Tanner smashed into Tanner's boat with tremendous force, sending men, weapons and supplies flying everywhere.

Suddenly, the air was filled with war cries. On the cables suspended above the reef, dozens of Keyowah warriors slid down from the cliffs on either side of the bay. The cables ran directly above the ruined boats. The Keyowah warriors, primed and ready for battle, dropped right into the middle of the Wallace men. Like berserkers, they tore through their enemy. The Wallace men, reeling from the bone-breaking collisions only seconds gone, rallied as best they could, but they didn't stand a chance. The overwhelming ferocity of the Keyowah decided the outcome, and by the time Caleb and his men scrambled out of the water to join the fighting, the battle was over. The decks of the shattered boats were littered with the dead and the dying.

The few remaining Wallace men dropped their weapons and surrendered as soon as Caleb reached the main deck.

While the Keyowah rounded up the prisoners, Tasi walked across the deck toward Caleb, Masu, and Samuel. He wiped blood out of his eyes, issuing orders to his men as he went. The Keyowah began taking defensible positions, eyeing the three remaining Wallace boats out on the open ocean.

Caleb scanned the deck, taking in everything: the condition of the ship, the few men he had left, and the dwindling ammunition supplies. The assessment brought a grimace to his face.

Tasi saw the look and smiled. "You didn't really think you would live forever, did you, brother?" he asked.

Caleb returned the smile. "Do you have anyone on the cliffs?"

Tasi nodded. "I do," he responded. "Always." He focused on the Wallace boats. "But those guns will ensure that we do not see tomorrow."

Caleb stared hard at the Wallace shielded .50s. "Damn his eyes," he said.

Samuel stepped forward. "We can still give him a fight, can't we, Caleb?" he asked.

"If he has free range with those .50s, Sam," Caleb answered, "it'll be like shooting at paper targets."

Samuel glanced from Caleb to Tasi to Masu, as if searching for something hopeful, some encouraging word. Caleb gave his younger brother a somber nod.

"But, yes, we can still give him a fight, Sam. Tavingtons always go loud."

Caleb knelt down behind the deck rail, pulled the pistol out of his blood-soaked waistband and checked it. Masu, Tasi and Samuel hunkered down beside him. Tasi grabbed a nearby rifle and slid another to Masu.

Caleb looked over at Tasi. "It's a nice day for it, brother," he said.

Tasi smiled a devil's smile. "It is that," he agreed. "The mother is kind, to allow us to die together, in the sunshine."

Caleb checked the group's readiness. He nodded at Masu, then gave Samuel an almost apologetic look. Samuel, however, took a deep breath, his eyes steady, even confident.

"It's a nice day for it, brother," he said.

Caleb smiled, and there was a glint of pride in his eyes. "It is that," he replied. Caleb signaled to one of his men nearby. "Kelloran," he said. "See if you can get this tin can running and slide us back out of this mess."

Kelloran disappeared below deck at a sprint. Soon, the engines coughed and sputtered and the ship began to rock back and forth on the wreckage of the ship it was half-buried in.

On the far horizon, the five ships commanded by Clay Abelard appeared and sped full throttle toward them. Seeing them, Tasi laughed softly.

Samuel turned to Masu. "You wouldn't have an extra smoke, would you, Masu? Hate to go never having tried one."

Caleb squinted his eyes at the arriving Wallace reinforcements. "Those boats don't look like they've just been hit by .50 fire, do they, Tas?" he asked.

Tasi shook his head. "No."

Caleb considered for a moment. "Clay must have found religion, staring into those big barrels at the bottom of the cliff."

Masu handed Samuel a cigarette, put one in his own mouth, and lit both.

The Wallace yachts, now numbering eight, motored toward Caleb and his men.

The ship's engine whined and roared as Kelloran attempted to break them free from the wreckage of the crushed boat beneath it. The sound of creaking, splintering wood filled the air.

Just outside of .50-cal range, the Wallace boats stopped.

• • • •

On the bridge of the lead boat, Black Wallace stared out of the window at the remaining Tavington force and barked out a laugh.

"Trapped on burning ships in the middle of a reef," he crowed. "Well done, Tavington. Welcome to your funeral." Black picked up the radio.

At that moment, Michael entered the bridge, radio in hand, strangely calm.

"Congratulations, Father," he said in a soft voice. "You appear to have the upper hand."

"Where the hell have you been, boy?" Black growled.

"I wanted to make sure you had a proper audience for your victory." Michael set his radio down on the map table.

"What are you talking about?" Black asked, and it was clear by his demeanor that he had no patience left for his son.

Michael smiled, and on his drawn face, it looked like a death's head grin. "Look around, Father," he said.

Black scanned the ocean. A large group of ships had appeared on the horizon and were advancing on their position at speed.

"What the hell have you done?" Black asked, his eyes narrowing.

Michael didn't answer right away. Instead, he focused on the incoming boats, each one clearly prepped for battle, with all hands on deck and soldiers manning the .50-cal guns.

"Hmm," he finally responded in a quiet voice. "Destroying the Tavingtons is really none of their concern, Father, but the Council was very interested in your generous sharing of the map book with your rebel friends."

The meaning of his son's words slowly dawned on Black Wallace, hammered home by the twenty battle boats rapidly approaching. The fury in his eyes was terrible to see, but Michael didn't seem to be concerned at all.

"You worthless…," Black began, voice thick with anger. "You have no idea what you've done. You've betrayed your own family."

Michael stared his father straight in the eye. "You are a traitor and a coward," he said, "and you're no family of mine." With that, Michael turned and walked toward the exit door.

"You miserable ingrate," Black screamed at Michael's back. "You're pathetic. You're a disgrace. Do you think they'll thank you for this? Shake your hand? The Tavingtons will grind you into sand. They'll take it all away, you—"

Michael spun suddenly, pistol in hand, pointed at his father's face. "I could kill you now," he said. His breath came in short gasps, as if from a hard run. "I've practiced it thousands of times. I've even dreamt about it." He cocked the hammer back.

"Go ahead," Black said. "If you think you are man enough, go ahead." He stepped menacingly forward, gauging the distance to Michael.

Michael swallowed hard, his knuckles white from their vise grip on the pistol. He sucked in a deep breath, and his finger tightened on the trigger. Black stopped moving and braced himself for the shot.

Michael relaxed his hand. He exhaled a long, trembling breath. "You'd like that, wouldn't you? The quick way out." He shook his head. "No, I think I'll let Council decide the manner and time of your passing. I'm actually looking forward to it. We haven't had a good hanging in the Archipelago for years."

* * * *

Across the water, on the deck of the ruined yacht, Caleb and the others watched the armada of Council battle boats pull in around Black Wallace's yacht, the flags of the four remaining families flying high in the Archipelago sunshine.

"What's going on?" Samuel asked.

Caleb shook his head.

By this time, Kelloran had managed to move the boat back through the gap, scraping reef all along the way. The hull was damaged, taking water and listing side to side, but the ship limped off the reef and into open ocean.

Caleb signaled the bridge and the boat motored slowly toward Black's yacht. As they made their final approach, the stairwell door on the Wallace yacht opened and Michael led Black out onto the deck, his pistol jammed into the back of his father's head.

Caleb's boat slid roughly alongside the Kench yacht, facing the Wallaces. On the Kench yacht, Warwicke stood tall in the middle of the deck. Once the Tavington vessel had come to a grinding halt, Warwicke began reading from a piece of paper.

"Council cannot ignore the charge brought against you by your own son, Eamon," Warwicke announced, loud enough that everyone on the Tavington, Kench and Wallace boats could hear. "You have been accused of breaking the code."

Caleb's eyes were fixed hard on Black Wallace. The Tavington ship had jammed its way between the Kench and Smythe yachts, and in doing so had slid so far forward that its bow was only feet from the Wallace bow.

Oblivious to Warwicke and everything else, Caleb walked all the way to the very edge of his bow. The only thing that seemed to matter to him at this moment was Black Wallace.

Samuel also made the walk, to stand just beside his brother. The cigarette from Masu dangled on his lips.

Warwicke paused in his reading. "Stand down, Caleb," he said. "Wallace is marked by Council."

Caleb ignored Warwicke completely. He and Black Wallace stared each other down, years of hatred and the specter of Alistair Tavington's murder condensed into the space between them. It was like a living thing, snapping and clawing at the two of them, forcing them to the edge of a cliff.

Black tilted his head back arrogantly. "Challenge," he called out with a disdainful sneer.

Warwicke jerked his head back, surprised. "The accused has no right to challenge," Warwicke said. "Caleb has no obligation—"

"Accepted." Caleb's voice cut Warwicke off.

Without hesitation, Caleb took the pistol out of his waistband and handed it to Samuel. He stepped up on the bow rail, leaped the distance to the Wallace yacht, and landed in a tight roll. His eyes were immediately up and refocused on Black. From his crouch, he straightened slowly to a full standing position.

For a heavy moment, the tableau was frozen into place. Nobody moved or made a sound. Warwicke seemed unable to comprehend what was going on and managed only a confused look, his jaws working soundlessly as if he was searching for the right words. Even the sounds of the ocean seemed muted in this moment, with Caleb Tavington and Black Wallace poised to settle their bitter feud once and for all time.

Black Wallace smiled, rolled his neck side to side, then made as if to step toward Caleb. Instead, however, he whirled around, slamming his body into Michael's. In a blur, he hammered his forearm down onto Michael's wrist, disarming him and taking the pistol. A hard elbow under Michael's rib cage pushed Black clear, and he spun, bringing the pistol to bear on Caleb.

The movement was so brutal and quick, and Michael's resistance so weak, that it was only a lightning-flash moment before Caleb was caught, unarmed, standing under the gun of Black Wallace. There was no defense possible, no shelter in reach, and no time at all to counter.

Caleb simply lifted his head without fear as Black lined the pistol up on his chest.

The bang of a gunshot echoed across the otherwise silent Archipelago ocean, immediately followed by a second.

Black Wallace jerked and flew backwards into Michael, as if a giant hand had simply swatted him away.

Caleb turned slowly.

Near the bow rail of the Tavington yacht stood Samuel, face pale, Caleb's smoking gun in his hand. His eyes were locked on Black Wallace's body, now pooling blood in a crumpled heap on the deck. After a few silent seconds, he lifted his head and met Caleb's eyes.

On the Kench yacht, Warwicke remained stock-still, staring at Samuel, the paper he was reading from forgotten in his hand.

Caleb looked over. "I don't think you'll need to finish reading those charges, Warwicke," he said, an edge of finality in his voice.

Warwicke let the paper go, and the wind took it high into the air and out into the ocean.

CHAPTER FIFTEEN

The Archipelago sun pushed through the early-morning fog, sending its first rays out into the chill of the fleeing night. The horizon lightened, purple to pink to orange, signaling to the denizens of this ocean wilderness that a new day had come. Seabirds took to the skies in search of the day's adventure.

Below them, a gleaming yacht cut across the surface of the calm blue water, humming at full speed toward the breaking dawn. At the ship's wheel, Samuel steered a smooth course with natural ease, relaxed and calm. There was about him a confidence that would have seemed out of place in the youngster who had stepped off the boat ramp from Harvard not long before.

A dark shape on the horizon quickly became a cargo freighter, and Samuel adjusted his course toward it. Soon, the freighter was close enough to read the lettering on its hull. Samuel smiled and reduced his speed as the vessel's name caught the early-morning sunlight. It was the Marchana Line freighter, the *St. Christopher*. Once the Tavington yacht was within twenty yards of the cargo ship, Samuel idled the engines.

"Passo," he said. "Take over, if you please."

"Aye," Passo replied, stepping forward from the rear of the bridge and taking the wheel.

Samuel patted Passo on the back and headed for the stairs.

• • • •

Samuel walked out of the stairwell onto the deck. On the far rail, three of the Tavington men docked the boat against the hull of the *St. Christopher*. Almost hidden in the shadow of the large freighter,

Caleb and Emma stood waiting at the bow, two large suitcases at their feet. They smiled at Samuel's approach.

Above them, a rope ladder platform descended from the *St. Christopher*. Caleb and Emma stepped back as the platform settled onto the deck in front of them, and Caleb loaded the suitcases onto the rigging.

• • • •

Moments later, Caleb, Emma and Samuel stood on the deck of the *St. Christopher* with the merchant ship captain, Zoo Cali.

"Thank you, Zoo," Caleb said. "I know you don't normally take passengers."

Zoo smiled, revealing brand-new gold caps. "Please," he answered, "say no more. I am honored beyond measure. My men will see to the bags." He bowed and, with a wink at Samuel, backed away.

Caleb turned to Samuel. "Goodbye, Sam," he said, a look of deep affection on his face.

"Goodbye, Caleb," Samuel responded, and there were tears in his eyes. "I can't tell you how much I...you've been..."

Caleb smiled and put his hands on Samuel's shoulders. "You will be the best of all of us, Sam," he said. "You will be the finest Tavington yet, mark my words."

The tears began to roll down Samuel's face. "I'll miss you, Caleb. I really will."

"You're going to be fine, Sam...just fine." Caleb nodded to his younger brother and stepped back. As he did, Emma rushed in, threw her arms around Samuel, and squeezed tight.

• • • •

On the horizon, the morning sun settled into its work, its rays already producing heat waves in the near distance. As the Archipelago began to feel the warmth of the coming day, the Marchana freighter separated from the Tavington yacht. Both ship's engines roared to life and they swung wide in their reversals, putting a frothy wake between them.

The *St. Christopher* boomed its foghorn loudly in farewell, then once again as the big engines kicked into gear and motored away.

The Tavington yacht reversed well clear of the freighter's wake, then spun neatly and sped in the opposite direction.

· · · ·

On the bridge of the Tavington yacht, Passo remained at the wheel. He glanced back at the *St. Christopher*. "Godspeed," he said softly.

At the bridge window, Caleb stood with Emma, watching the big ship silhouetted against the horizon. On the deck of the freighter, Samuel stared back toward them. He lifted his hand in a wave.

"Godspeed," Caleb said. He put his arm around Emma. "I'm sorry, Em," he whispered, just loud enough for her to hear.

Emma looked up at Caleb.

"I made a promise to you," he continued, "and I—"

"You are Caleb Tavington," Emma interrupted, "and you did what you have always done...the right thing."

Caleb's eyes remained fixed on the *St. Christopher*, like a drowning man watching a life raft float just out of his reach. "Maybe someday," he said.

Emma nodded. "Maybe...but this is the life we were born to, Caleb. It's the life that was thrust upon us. For better or worse, this is the life we lead."

Caleb exhaled slowly. "The mother chooses," he sighed, voice resigned. "It's not up to us."

They stared out at the endless sky, at the vast expanse of wild blue ocean that surrounded them. Even the Marchana freighter seemed suddenly small, dwarfed by the magnitude of the Archipelago.

"Samuel might not belong in the Archipelago," she said, "but you do, Caleb. We do...and that's good enough."

Caleb nodded in acknowledgment, then turned resolutely away from the *St. Christopher*. He focused his eyes firmly forward, jaw set, as they sped back into the heart of the Archipelago.

Emma lowered her voice as she added, in a whisper, "For now."

Caleb shot a quick glance down at her and raised his eyebrow, the ghost of a smile flickering across his face.

Emma smiled in response, blinking back tears. She reached her arms around Caleb and hugged him tight.

• • • •

THE END

If you enjoyed BLOOD-FEUD and have a moment, please leave a review at your online book retailer of choice. Reviews are more important to authors than you might think, and your honest opinion will help other readers discover the Lords of the Archipelago.

I _really_ appreciate your support.

Thank you!

One final thing...

Book Two of the Lords of the Archipelago series is in the works and will be rolling out soon.

To receive Archipelago updates along with information about upcoming release dates, sign up for my email list. I won't bug you and you'll be in the loop.

You can sign up here: www.authordbmotu.com[1]

Just scroll down to the bottom of the page, type in your email address and you're set for any and all future Archipelago updates.

Welcome to the Archipelago!

---

1. http://www.authordbmotu.com

About the Author

D.B. Motu is a recovering screenwriter, often found drowning in coffee shops. He was born on an island you've never heard of and grew up under martial law in Southeast Asia. He insists he's directly descended from Samoan and British royalty, and counts among his ancestors a South Seas pirate. He's a board-gaming poet and aspiring liar. Pull up a chair.

Read more at https://www.authordbmotu.com.

www.ingramcontent.com/pod-product-compliance
Lightning Source LLC
Chambersburg PA
CBHW021200160726
47994CB00001B/305